Great Moments in
BASKETBALL
HISTORY

MATT CHRISTOPHER®

THE #1 SPORTS SERIES FOR KIDS

Great Moments in
BASKETBALL
HISTORY

Text by Stephanie Peters

LITTLE, BROWN AND COMPANY
New York ● Boston

Little, Brown Books for Young Readers

Hachette Book Group
237 Park Avenue, New York, NY 10017
Visit our Web site at www.lb-kids.com

www.mattchristopher.com

Little, Brown and Company is a division of Hachette Book Group, Inc.
The Little, Brown name and logo are trademarks of Hachette Book Group, Inc.

First Edition: October 2009

Matt Christopher® is a registered trademark of
Matt Christopher Royalties, Inc.

Text written by Stephanie Peters

Library of Congress Cataloging-in-Publication Data

Christopher, Matt.
    Great moments in basketball history / Matt Christopher. —1st ed.
        p.   cm.
    ISBN 978-0-316-04483-7
    1. Basketball — United States — History — Juvenile literature.   2. Basketball players — United States — History — Juvenile literature.   3. National Basketball Association — History — Juvenile literature.   I. Title.
    GV885.1.C47 2009
    796.323 — dc22

                                                    2008049176

10 9 8 7 6 5 4 3 2 1

CW

Printed in the United States of America

Contents

Great Moments in
BASKETBALL
HISTORY

⋆ INTRODUCTION ⋆

DECEMBER 1891

Basketball Is Born

No book about great moments in basketball history would be complete without mentioning the greatest achievement of all: the creation of the sport itself! Unlike many popular sports that evolved gradually from existing games, basketball sprang from one man's imagination.

James A. Naismith was a physical education instructor at the International Young Men's Christian Association Training School in Springfield, Massachusetts, in 1891. Chief among his duties was to lead classes through daily indoor exercise routines. Those routines included marching, calisthenics, and games like leapfrog.

Many students didn't want to do these boring and childish activities, however. They were used to competitive sports like baseball and football — activities that challenged them physically and mentally and were exciting, too. They found jumping jacks and somersaults to be poor substitutes and demanded a new indoor activity.

So Naismith tried to adapt existing sports to the indoor arena instead. His attempts failed miserably.

"We tried to play football indoors, but that broke the arms and legs of the players," Naismith recalled. "We then tried soccer, but broke all the windows. Then we tried lacrosse, and broke up the apparatus."

Naismith tried to figure out why the sports hadn't worked indoors. Football had failed, he decided, because players were hurt when they were tackled while running with the ball. If players weren't allowed to run with the ball, then they wouldn't get hurt.

So how was a player to move the ball if he couldn't run with it? His indoor soccer experiment had proved that kicking the ball wouldn't work. Arming players with sticks like those used in lacrosse or hockey struck him as too dangerous.

What if the ball was passed from teammate to teammate? Tackling would be illegal, but a player could bat the ball away in midflight and capture it for himself. Injuries would be much less likely to occur if the defense focused on the ball and not the player.

2

Next Naismith turned his attention to how points should be scored. With the exception of baseball, most sports featured two goals set up at opposite ends of a playing field. They all used the same general scoring method: power an object past a goalkeeper with as much speed and force as possible to earn a point.

Naismith liked the idea of opposing goals, but in his opinion — and recent experience — power, force, and speed were too dangerous for confined, indoor play. So instead of players hurling the ball *laterally* toward a goal protected by a player at ground level, he decided they would toss it *vertically* toward an untended goal mounted up high. Skill and accuracy, not power, would earn points, and no one player would be responsible for preventing goals.

From these starting points, Naismith came up with thirteen general rules for his new game. He posted those rules on the YMCA's gymnasium door in late December of 1891. He nailed a peach basket — the first hoops — at each end of a railing that circled the gym floor. The railing was ten feet above the floor, and to this day, that is the height at which basketball hoops are hung.

Basketball was an immediate hit with Naismith's students. Soon other local YMCAs adopted the sport and formed teams that played against one another. Slowly, but surely, basketball spread to colleges and universities, where it was played by both men and women. Communities rented out their dance halls and barns to those looking for a place to play. While the heart of the sport beat most powerfully in the Northeast, traveling teams, called barnstormers, introduced the game to far-flung corners of the country — and beyond.

Basketball became an Olympic sport — played by twenty-three nations, including Japan, Italy, and Brazil — during the Berlin Games in 1936. The United States won the gold, the first of many basketball gold medals it would win in the decades that followed.

Meanwhile, professional leagues sprouted up throughout the United States. After the failed National Basketball League (NBL) of the 1890s came the American Basketball League (ABL). First organized in 1925, the ABL remained in existence in one form or another until 1955. A new NBL, a smaller-scale version of the ABL, was established in 1937. In 1948, it merged with yet another league, the Basketball Association of America (BAA) to form a brand-new organization, the National Basketball Association — today's NBA. The American Basketball Association (ABA) was developed eighteen years later and would compete with the NBA for talent and fans until its demise in 1976.

That left the NBA as the sole men's professional basketball league in the United States. There are minor leagues, most notably the Continental Basketball Association (CBA) and the United States Basketball League (USBL), as well as a professional women's league, the Women's National Basketball Association (WNBA). These three organizations have vaulted the sport of basketball to tremendous new heights, as has the National Collegiate Athletic Association (NCAA).

But when it comes to professional basketball in the United States, the NBA stands alone. It is home to some of the greatest teams in sports history, as well as current teams bursting with talent. It boasts charismatic players whose careers are discussed with admiration and awe and whose signature moves are imitated on courts around the world.

It would be impossible to highlight every great moment in basketball history in the pages of one book; there have simply been too many. That's why in the chapters that follow, only a small selection of the most dazzling displays of professional basketball talent are replayed.

James Naismith once said, "I want to leave the world a little bit better than I found it." As anyone who has taken a shot at a hoop, dribbled a ball, or bounced a pass would agree, he achieved his goal — and more.

★ MAY 5, 1957 ★

BILL RUSSELL

The Rookie Blocks the Shot

Bill Russell was the first, and arguably greatest, master of the blocked shot. In the course of his NBA career, the Boston Celtics center denied hundreds of opponents with a quick and powerful flick of his hand. But one block, like Russell himself, stands head and shoulders above the rest.

Russell joined the Celtics in December of 1956. He was brought to the team by a feisty, cigar-chomping coach named Red Auerbach. Auerbach had put together a dynamic team that included point guard Bob Cousy, still considered by many to be the best playmaker ever, as well as future Hall of Famers Bill Sharman, Frank Ramsey, and Jim Loscutoff.

But before Russell came on board, Auerbach felt that his team lacked some crucial element, something that would vault the Celtics from good to great. Then he saw Bill Russell play and knew he'd found what was missing: defense!

Today, defensive tactics such as blocking shots and rebounding are just a part of the game. But back then, no one bothered to put much thought into defense. No one but Russell, that is.

Russell was a self-taught student of basketball defense. He studied an opponent's offensive style — where on the floor a player liked to shoot from, what kind of shot he liked to take, and how he took it. Then he used that knowledge, plus his speed, height, and agility, to put himself between the shooter and the basket, to deflect the shot away from the mark, and to send the ball into the waiting hands of his own teammate.

"Defense is an action, not a reaction," Russell said years later. "Great defense attacks an opponent's offense versus reacting to it."

It was a simple enough concept, but as Russell once commented, "I knew, absolutely, that ninety-nine percent of people watching me play had no idea what I was doing."

But Russell knew what he was doing, and exactly why he was doing it. He believed that games were won by the defense, and that championships were won when the whole team worked together to build a defense equal in strength to its offense.

He put his concept into action during his debut game on December 22, 1956. The Celtics were playing the St. Louis Hawks for the fourth time that season. Boston had won the three previous games, but the scores had been close. That night's score was also close, with Boston putting up 95 points and St. Louis 93.

But the tables might very well have been turned if not for Bill Russell. He came off the bench midway through the game. Offensively, he wasn't a threat; in the twenty-one minutes he was on the court, he scored just six points. Defensively, however, he ripped down 16 rebounds. More importantly, he blocked three shots attempted by the Hawks' star forward-center, Bob Pettit, late in the fourth quarter.

That was no easy task, for Pettit was a scoring machine who would later become the first player in history to reach the 20,000-point mark. But that night, he was the first player to feel the effects of Russell's mighty defense. He wasn't the last.

As the season wore on, Russell denied countless points. No one knows exactly how many, because at the time blocks were not recorded in the statistics —

proof enough that few people considered them important! But by routinely preventing points and chalking up numbers in the rebound column, Russell helped the Celtics to a league-high regular season record of 44 wins and 28 losses.

Boston sweetened their win numbers in the postseason by sweeping the Syracuse Nationals in three straight games in the playoff semifinals. They advanced to the championship round, where they faced the Hawks.

The Hawks were coming off a five-game postseason winning streak. They continued that streak by beating the Celtics 125–123 in the first game of the Finals. That match went into double overtime. It might have gone on to an unprecedented third overtime had not Atlanta's Jack Coleman sunk a long bomb just as the clock ran out.

Boston roared back the next night, however, with a score of 119–99. That victory was thanks in large part to Bill Russell, who held Bob Pettit to just eleven points.

The series moved to St. Louis for game three. The two teams battled furiously, each hoping to break the tie in their favor. In the final minutes, the score was knotted at 98 apiece. Then Pettit got the ball and launched a jump shot. The ball hit cleanly — and the game ended with a score of 100–98.

Pettit was his team's high scorer again the next game, with a total of thirty-three points. But the Celtics' star guard, Bob Cousy, matched him almost point for point, and when his Boston teammates drained more total baskets than Pettit's, the Celtics had another mark in their "win" column. They added another before their adoring hometown fans in Boston to go ahead in the series three games to two. One more victory, and the Celtics would be crowned the NBA champs.

The win didn't come the following game, however. The Finals were back in St. Louis for game six. The last thing the Hawks wanted was to fall short in front of their fans. So they threw everything they had at the Celtics.

Boston fought back with just as much ferocity. As the minutes ticked by, the score seesawed back and forth between the evenly matched teams. Then, with twelve seconds left to play and the score tied at 94 apiece, Cousy came to the foul line. He bounced the ball, took aim, shot — and missed!

With one chance to pull ahead for the win, the Hawks got the ball to Pettit. Pettit unleashed a shot

11

a split second before the buzzer sounded. As the ball arced gracefully through the air, the Hawks and their fans held their breath. The Celtics, meanwhile, willed the ball to veer off course.

It didn't. When it passed cleanly through the net, the Hawks had another win in their pockets. St. Louis fans went wild, the Hawks celebrated — and the Celtics trudged to the locker room to lick their wounds and prepare for the final and decisive seventh game.

The Boston Garden was teeming with Celtics fans the night of game seven. Those who couldn't be there in person listened to the play-by-play on the radio, given by the Celtics' new announcer, Johnny Most, whose gravelly voice and excited commentary would soon become legendary.

Boston took control early in the game but couldn't hold the lead. The first quarter ended with the score 28–26 in favor of St. Louis. The Celtics raced ahead at the start of the second only to falter as the half wound down.

Boston struggled to hold their advantage after halftime. Then, as the final minutes clicked by, the Hawks swooped down and stole the lead. With two minutes left, St. Louis jumped up by four. Boston clawed its way back, however, sinking three free throws to come within one. Still . . .

Tick, tick, tick! Time was running out. The Celtics had possession. They launched an attack, hoping to add two with a Cousy-to-Russell basket.

But Russell's shot attempt failed. His forward momentum propelled him over the baseline and out-of-bounds, leaving the remaining four Celtics to fight the Hawks for the rebound.

The Hawks came down with the ball and quickly fed an outlet pass to Jack Coleman — the same player who had hit the game-winning double-overtime shot in game one. Coleman stood alone at midcourt. The moment the ball hit his hands, he took off for the basket.

What happened next was, in the words of teammate Bob Cousy, "the most incredible physical act I've ever seen on a basketball floor."

Bill Russell took off running from behind the baseline like he'd been shot out of a cannon. His strides were so long and his pace was so quick that he covered ninety-four yards of court to arrive at the hoop at the exact moment Coleman went up for his layup! And then . . .

WHAP! He knocked the ball away!

"Blocked by Russell! Blocked by Russell! He came from nowhere!" Johnny Most screamed, his voice raw with emotion.

Russell didn't just block the ball, however — he controlled it. And then he turned and dribbled it madly toward the other end. Seconds later, he scored! And when Cousy drained a free throw, Boston had a two-point lead!

Yet, unbelievably, they couldn't keep it. Pettit was fouled going up for a shot and sank both free throws to send the game into overtime. The score was *still* tied at the end of those minutes, forcing a second overtime.

It had been a long, exhausting, and emotionally draining match for both teams. But all games come to an end at some point, with one team the winner and one the loser. This time, it was the Boston Celtics who emerged triumphant to win their first-ever NBA championship, 125–123.

The victory had been a team effort, of course, but everyone agreed that Bill Russell's court-length charge had given the Celtics the chance they needed to win. If he hadn't made that monumental effort to deny Coleman those two points, the Hawks might very easily have won. Russell had also helped by crashing the boards for a rookie record of 32 rebounds, bringing his Finals average to 22.9 for the series.

How did the Celtics reward their rookie center, the man who, in the words of Coach Auerbach, "single-handedly revolutionized this game simply because he made defense so important"? In a jubilant display of team spirit, they shaved his beard in the locker room!

Bill Russell remained with the Celtics for thirteen seasons as a player, the last three as a player-coach alongside Red Auerbach. During his career, Boston won an unprecedented eleven championships. Russell was named the NBA's Most Valuable Player five times. He retired in 1969 and is considered by basketball followers to be one of the most influential players the game has ever seen.

WILT CHAMBERLAIN

100

"Give it to Wilt! Give it to Wilt!"

The chant rang out through the small basketball arena in rural Hershey, Pennsylvania, a town better known for its chocolate than its sports. But on March 2, 1962, Hershey would take its place in the record books as the site of one of the greatest achievements in NBA history. It was there that Wilt Chamberlain of the Philadelphia Warriors did what no player before or since has done.

At seven feet one inch tall and 275 pounds, Chamberlain was a big man among a league of big men and was the most dominant offensive player of the era. During the 1961–62 season, he was well on his way to averaging more than 50 points per game. In one five-week period, he had the two highest-scoring games on record. On December 8, he racked up a record-shattering 78-point total in a triple-overtime victory against Los Angeles. And then, on January 13, he posted 73 points in the 135–117 win over the Chicago Packers, the greatest total ever in regulation play.

Some believed those impressive numbers would remain untouched for many years to come. But others, including Philadelphia's coach, Frank McGuire, often speculated that Chamberlain would reach the 100-point mark before his career ended. Reaching that goal wouldn't be easy, however.

"Think just what it takes to score that much," McGuire once pointed out. "Why, if you or I went to the gym alone it would take us almost half an hour to make enough for one hundred points."

But what, exactly, was the most celebrated center in the NBA doing in Hershey, Pennsylvania? He and the Warriors were there to face the New York Knicks. Usually, the teams played in either Philadelphia or New York, but the NBA had seen a drop in its attendance recently. Hoping to boost its fan base beyond the populations of big cities, it had scheduled the match at the out-of-the-way site.

Unfortunately, the tactic didn't work. The 8,000-seat arena was only half full at game time. Hardly any newspaper reporters or photographers showed up either. And there was only one radio announcer and no television crew.

Because of this, almost no media coverage of the match exists today. In fact, there is only one known recording of the original radio broadcast of the historic game. That recording was made by a college student who held his tape player up to his radio and then put the tape away after the game and forgot about it — for almost thirty years!

Of course, no one knew that Wilt "the Stilt" Chamberlain would make basketball history that night. Those who saw Wilt hours before the game might have wondered if he was even thinking about basketball at all. He was in a local penny arcade, playing pinball and taking aim at targets in the shooting gallery.

Interestingly, Chamberlain traces the start of his magical performance to that little arcade. He was playing the games for fun, and yet, deep down, he realized something else was happening.

"It seemed like whatever I touched, I was breaking record after record," he recalled later. "I just knew I was on. I completely destroyed all existing shooting records there — an omen of things to come."

A few hours later, Chamberlain had traded an air rifle for a basketball. He warmed up with the rest of the Warriors and then took his place in the center circle for the opening tip-off. He faced the Knicks' backup center, Darrell Imhoff, who was starting in place of his ailing teammate, Phil Jordan. The ref blew his whistle and tossed the ball up in the air between the two men. The game was on.

Moments after the tip-off, Chamberlain got the ball and tossed it through the hoop for his first two points of the game. By the end of the first quarter, he had drained six more baskets in thirteen attempts for 14 points. He had also shot nine for nine from the free throw line, an unheard-of streak for him. His usual free throw average hovered closer to 50 percent, not 100!

Thanks to Chamberlain's 23 points, as well as his 10 rebounds, the Warriors ended the first quarter ahead of the Knicks, 42–26. Wilt drove the offense in the second quarter, too, boosting his own game total to 41 and his team's to 79 by halftime.

Forty-one points in twenty-four minutes? The people in the stands buzzed with excitement. Would they witness the Big Dipper matching — or even beating — his own scoring record? As the halftime break came to an end, a few more photographers showed up, having received word that something major was happening at Hershey Arena.

The score stood at Warriors 79, Knicks 68 when the game resumed. An 11-point lead is sizable, but not insurmountable. The Knicks knew by then that to win the game, they would have to do one thing: shut down Chamberlain.

They couldn't. Double-, triple-, and even the occasional *quadruple*-team defenses against the Warriors' center made no difference at all. Wilt was on fire, and the Warriors fed the flames, passing him the ball time and again and then standing back to watch him sink shots from all over the floor.

"There wasn't an easier way in the world to get assists tonight," said Warrior Guy Rodgers, who earned 20 in that stat column that night. "All I had to do was give the ball to the Dipper."

"It was like holding up a tree that had been cut and was about to fall down," Imhoff commented later about Chamberlain's unrelenting offensive attack. "My sneakers were smoking."

The Knicks tried another tactic that had worked against Wilt before — they fouled him, trusting that he would miss more free throws than he made and give them the chance to snare the rebounds. And on other nights, that strategy might have succeeded.

But that night, he drained free throw after free throw. By the end of the third quarter, he had scored an unbelievable 69 points, 21 of which had come from the foul line. The Warriors had a commanding lead of 125–109. But by that time, few people cared about the outcome of the game. They were too busy focusing on Chamberlain.

"Here's the big fourth quarter," broadcaster Bill Campbell announced at the start of the final twelve minutes of play, "and everybody is thinking, How many is Wilt gonna get?"

Chamberlain needed just four points to match his own regulation game record of 73, five to beat it. *Swish! Swish! Swish!* Three baskets and less than two minutes later, he had jumped from 69 points to 75!

The crowd was going wild, filling the arena with their whistles, cheers, and chants. Their frenzied excitement grew even greater when, with 7:51 left to play, Chamberlain lofted a jump shot from the foul line to make his 79th point of the game.

It had taken him forty-eight minutes of regulation

play and fifteen minutes of overtime to reach 78 points just three months earlier. This night, it had taken him barely forty minutes to make 79!

By this time, the Knicks had thrown almost every trick in the book at Chamberlain in their desperate attempt to stop him from scoring. They knew the game was lost; now they were fighting for their dignity. They didn't want to be forever known as the team that allowed one player to score one hundred points!

So, despite the fact that they were behind in the score, the Knicks started to run down the twenty-four-second shot clock whenever they had the ball. They hoped the game would end before Chamberlain could reach the triple-digit mark. When they didn't have possession, they fouled every Warrior except Wilt, hoping to break his streak.

But nothing they did could stop him. Dave Zinkoff, the Warriors' public address announcer, counted off Chamberlain's mounting point total for the audience. "That's eighty-one," he bellowed, as Wilt sank yet another bucket. When he called out, "That's eighty-nine!" there were still more than five minutes left to go!

One hundred points was within reach. But time

was ticking down — and suddenly, Wilt stopped scoring. The Knicks' fouling tactic seemed to be working.

Coach McGuire wasn't about to sit by and let his star player be robbed of his chance at making history. So, with less than three minutes remaining, he sent in Joe Ruklick, Ted Luckenbill, and York Larese with one simple set of instructions: foul the Knicks. Get the ball. Then pass to Wilt.

It worked. Chamberlain sank a free throw, his 90th point, with 2:45 on the clock. He was fouled a moment later and racked up two more points on free throws. Then he tossed in a fadeaway that brought him to 94.

Six points to go! He looked poised to get two more when Rodgers fed him the ball near the hoop. Wilt bobbled the pass — but then recovered the ball and arced yet another fadeaway into the hoop!

His next two points were made in spectacular fashion. Larese had the ball. Chamberlain was down low. He cut to the hoop, and Larese hit him with a high pass.

Slam! With 1:19 on the clock, Chamberlain stuffed that ball down the hoop's throat!

The fans were screaming themselves hoarse, and

as the sole surviving radio recording reveals, announcer Bill Campbell was right there with them.

"He has ninety-eight with 1:01 left, he can make it easily," the scratchy play-by-play rasps. "Rodgers in to Chamberlain, misses, Luckenbill rebound, pass to Chamberlain, misses again, Luckenbill rebound, back to Ruklick, in to Chamberlain . . . *he made it! He made it!* A Dipper dunk! He made it! . . . One hundred points for Wilt Chamberlain!"

Pandemonium broke out. There were still forty-six seconds left in the game, but for five minutes, all play stopped as the fans mobbed the court. Eventually, the game was finished, but the outcome was merely a sidebar to the night's main event.

Wilt had scored 100 points. He had shot 36-for-63 from the floor and 28-for-32 from the foul line. He once said that he was as proud of that second stat as he was of his 100-point total.

Remarkably, there are very few photos commemorating Chamberlain's historic feat. The most famous of these was snapped in the locker room after the game. Harvey Pollack, the Warriors' public relations man, grabbed a piece of paper, wrote the number 100 on it, and thrust it into Chamberlain's hands.

Wilt held it up and turned with an exhausted smile to the camera.

After all, making history is hard work.

Wilt Chamberlain played in the NBA for fourteen seasons. He was named league MVP four times, led the league in assists once, led in scoring seven times, and led in rebounding eleven times. He won his first championship in 1967 as a member of the Philadelphia 76ers and his second in 1972 with the Los Angeles Lakers. His 100-point record still stands today.

☆ APRIL 15, 1965 ☆

JOHN HAVLICEK

The Steal

Ask any basketball player what John "Hondo" Havlicek is best known for, and chances are they'll give similar answers: Endurance. Hustle. Staying power. "On stamina alone he'd be among the top players who ever played the game," an NBA coach once said of Havlicek.

"It's just a matter of pushing myself," Havlicek said. "I say to myself, 'He's as tired as I am. Who's going to win the mental battle?'"

Fortunately for the Boston Celtics, for whom Havlicek played all sixteen years of his career, he brought great scoring talent, ballhandling abilities, and tenacious defensive skills, along with his endurance and mental toughness. With these skills, he fit perfectly into the slot of "sixth man," the player teammates and coaches trust to come off the bench and help the team to victory.

"It's not who starts the game," Havlicek once replied when asked if he resented not being one of the starting five, "but who finishes it, and I generally was around to finish it."

The 1964–65 Celtics was a team of superstars. Veteran center Bill Russell dismantled offenses by blocking shots at will and turning rebounds into scoring opportunities. Guards K. C. Jones and Sam Jones put the plays in motion with lightning-quick passes and expert ballhandling. Forwards Tom Heinsohn and Tom "Satch" Sanders provided scoring and rebounding might.

Yet as strong as these five players were, they still needed someone capable of filling their shoes when they needed a break. That man was John Havlicek. When one of the guards or forwards stepped out, he stepped in and spurred on the attack.

As in the previous six years, the 1964–65 Celtics were virtually unstoppable. The team romped through the regular season to an amazing 62–18 record. In the early weeks, they won eleven games in a row before suffering a loss. Later, they bested that streak by winning sixteen consecutive games!

It was the Philadelphia 76ers who broke the

Celtics' streaks both times. The 1964–65 Sixers were a solid team, led by their newest acquisition: Wilt Chamberlain.

In fact, sparked by Chamberlain, the Sixers dealt the Celtics their greatest number of defeats that season. Out of the ten times the two teams met, five ended in losses for Boston. In comparison, the Los Angeles Lakers, the Baltimore Bullets, and the New York Knicks bested the Celtics three times each. The Cincinnati Royals won twice against Boston. The St. Louis Hawks and the San Francisco Warriors emerged victorious only once each. And the Detroit Pistons came up short every single time they played the Celtics that year!

To no one's surprise, the Celtics claimed the number-one spot in the Eastern Division. They faced the Sixers in the division finals after Philadelphia handily defeated the Cincinnati Royals. Whoever won the best-of-seven series now would advance to the NBA championship round against the winners of the Western Division.

Philadelphia hadn't been to the Finals since 1955, when they'd been known as the Syracuse Nationals. Chamberlain, despite being hailed as the greatest center in the NBA, had yet to win a championship ring. He and his teammates were hungry for a series win, but to do so, they'd have to beat the six-time reigning champs and their archrivals, the Boston Celtics.

The Celtics proved to be too powerful for the Sixers to handle in game one, with Boston winning 108–98. Game two was a different story — one that ended with the Sixers tying the series at one apiece before their cheering hometown fans. Boston took game three, 112–94, but once again, Philadelphia knotted things up by eking out a 134–131 win in overtime in game four. Games five and six duplicated the previous pairs, with each team winning one to send the series to the final, decisive seventh game.

Game seven took place in Boston Garden — an arena where so many opposing teams had lost that some players claimed it was cursed. Philadelphia players may have been justified in believing in that curse. After all, they had lost every game they'd played there that season!

But now, with the chance of advancing to the NBA Finals on the line, the Sixers were playing harder than ever before. The Celtics weren't about to bow down before their loyal fans, however, and battled with just as much ferocity.

The score seesawed back and forth as the clock ticked down to the final minutes. Then there were no minutes left, only seconds. With just five seconds remaining, the Celtics were up 110–107. Victory seemed certain.

But suddenly, Wilt Chamberlain got his hands on the ball and breezed to the basket for an easy layup! No Celtic stood in his way because no one wanted to foul him. But now the score stood at 110–109.

Celtic Bill Russell took the ball under the basket and prepared to inbound it to a teammate at the ref's whistle. All that teammate would have to do would be to hold on to the ball until the clock ran out. When he did, another trip to the Finals for Boston would be in the bag!

The whistle blew, Russell threw — and the unimaginable happened. Instead of traveling in a smooth arc over Chamberlain's outstretched arms and into a teammate's waiting hands, the ball struck one of the guide wires attached to Boston's basket! Now the Sixers had possession!

Five seconds may not seem like a long time, but in basketball, it is enough to get off one last shot. If that shot was taken by Chamberlain, there would be a very good chance of it going in. And if it did, then the 76ers, and not the Celtics, would be going on to the Finals.

Philadelphia guard Hal Greer took the ball out of bounds. The Celtics matched up man-to-man on defense. John Havlicek took up position near Sixer Chet Walker. He knew that once the ref handed the ball to Greer, Greer would have five seconds to put it in play.

"So I started to count to myself: one thousand one, one thousand two, one thousand three, one thousand four," Havlicek recounted years later. "When I got to one thousand four, I realized Greer was having a problem getting the ball in."

With one second remaining for the throw-in, Havlicek risked taking his eyes off Walker to glance at Greer. As he did, Greer lobbed a pass.

Havlicek leaped, stretched out his hand, and with one controlled sweep —

"*Havlicek steals it!*" Legendary radio announcer Johnny Most screamed into his microphone. "Over to Sam Jones. Havlicek stole the ball! It's all over! Johnny Havlicek stole the ball!"

Havlicek's quick reflexes may very well have saved the game — and the series — for the Celtics. If Greer had managed to get the ball in to Walker, or worse, Chamberlain, then Boston would have had few options. They could have let the receiver take the shot and hoped he missed or that his shot was blocked. Or they could have fouled the receiver to stop him from shooting, hoping he would miss his free throws and that they could grab the rebound.

Instead, Sam Jones got the ball and dribbled out the clock. The Celtics took the series and then went on to beat the Los Angeles Lakers, four games to one, to earn their seventh consecutive NBA title. All because, as Most so famously yelled, "Johnny Havlicek stole the ball!"

When John Havlicek retired in 1974, he held the NBA record for games played, was in the top ten for minutes played and total points, and had earned eight championship rings. But the greatest honor he received came from Red Auerbach. "If I had a son like John," Auerbach told a reporter at Havlicek's final game, "I'd be the happiest man in the world."

★ THE 1970 NBA FINALS ★

The Miracle and the Inspiration

In 1950, a man named Red Auerbach took the helm of the Boston Celtics and in less than a decade turned the team into the NBA's first dynasty. Behind his leadership, Boston won the Finals a record nine times from 1957 to 1966.

In 1967, another man named Red took the helm of a different team and in two years steered it straight past the Celtics and into NBA history. William "Red" Holzman took the job of head coach for the New York Knicks with one goal in mind: build a team that played together as a team. By 1969, he had accomplished that goal.

The cornerstone of the Knicks was Willis Reed. Originally placed in the forward position, Reed was moved to center in 1969. The center slot proved a perfect fit. Standing at six feet ten inches and weighing close to 240 pounds, Reed had the brawn to muscle his way inside. He was left-handed, making him difficult to defend once he found his way to the hoop. He had deadly shooting skills, too; he averaged nearly 20 or more points per game throughout his career. And to top it off, Reed had the ability to inspire his teammates to give every game their all.

Anchored by Reed and led by Holzman, the Knicks roared through the regular season to the Eastern Division's top rank with a record of 60 wins and only 22 losses. In November alone, they racked up eighteen wins in a row, the longest streak in the NBA at the time. They then powered their way through the early rounds of the playoffs, beating the Baltimore Bullets in seven games and the Milwaukee Bucks in five to advance to the Finals for the first time in the team's twenty-four-year history.

In the Western Division, meanwhile, the Los Angeles Lakers had made a surprising comeback to snare the opposing berth in the Finals. It had not been a smooth season for them, since their biggest players, Wilt Chamberlain and Elgin Baylor, had been sidelined in the early months with knee problems. Fortunately, the Lakers still had Jerry West, a guard whose precision passing, ballhandling, and shooting were equaled only by his drive to win.

That drive helped the Lakers claim second place in the division. With Chamberlain and Baylor back in the lineup, Los Angeles fought their way out of a 3–1 deficit to beat the Phoenix Suns in the first play-off round. The Lakers pounded the Atlanta Hawks in the semifinals, taking all four games, to make it to the championship round.

The Knicks and the Lakers met at New York's Madison Square Garden on April 24, 1970, for game one of the best-of-seven series. New York emerged victorious, 124–112, but Los Angeles tied things up by winning the second game, 105–103.

The teams traveled to the Forum in Los Angeles for game three. And what a game it was! The two evenly matched squads traded the lead throughout. With two minutes left in the fourth quarter, the score was knotted at 96 apiece. One minute forty-eight seconds later, it was still tied, each team having added four points to their side.

Twelve seconds remained. The Knicks prepared to inbound the ball from under the Lakers' basket. Their power forward Dave DeBusschere moved to set a pick so his teammate Bill Bradley could get the ball and shoot a jumper. But the pick didn't work.

Instead, DeBusschere got the ball. One head fake later, he tossed in a bucket to give New York a two-point lead.

Knicks fans were going wild. There were only three seconds left on the clock. The ball would be put into play from underneath New York's hoop. The Lakers were out of time-outs. There was no way Los Angeles could possibly score!

Or could they?

Wilt Chamberlain took the ball from the referee under the hoop. He passed it in to Jerry West, who nabbed the ball near the top of the key. One second ticked by. West put the ball to the floor and dribbled once, twice, three times — with Willis Reed right alongside him.

Another second ticked by. West reached a spot three feet shy of midcourt. Then, with just one second remaining, he launched the ball into the air toward the distant hoop.

"West throws it up . . . ," the Knicks' announcer, Bob Wolff, cried. His voice lingered over the airwaves just as the ball seemed to linger in the Forum's rafters.

The ball took so long to come down, in fact, that one player, Walt Frazier, had time to glance at West.

"The man's crazy," Frazier later remembered thinking. "He thinks it's really going to go in."

The arcing ball spun downward and, unbelievably, *went through the hoop*!

"*He makes it!*" Wolff shouted. "West threw it up and *makes it*!"

If that shot had been taken today, the Knicks would have won the game by a single point. That's because now if a basket is made from twenty-two feet or more from the hoop at the sidelines, or twenty-three feet nine inches or more from the top of the key, it counts as three points.

West's shot was made from sixty-three feet away! No one, before or since, has duplicated such a shot during a game situation. And the fact that West made it in the last second proves he deserved his nickname: "Mr. Clutch."

Sadly, Mr. Clutch's last-ditch effort did not result in victory for the Lakers that night. New York took the game in overtime, thanks in part to Reed, who made a foul shot to give the Knicks a one-point lead with less than a minute remaining. The final score was 111–108.

Game four of the series went into extra minutes as well, but this time, the Lakers emerged with the victory. The two teams met back in New York for the fifth game. The Lakers sprang ahead to take an early lead, but the Knicks weren't about to go down without a fight.

Then tragedy struck. Reed got the ball at the foul line. He made a move to dodge around Wilt Chamberlain. As he did, he tripped over Chamberlain's foot. Unable to stop himself, he fell to the floor, wrenching a muscle in his leg.

Pain shot through Reed. He rolled on the floor in agony, clutching his leg. The game stopped, and the crowd grew silent as Knicks fans realized that their star center was injured — badly.

With Reed out, the Knicks fell further behind. By halftime, they were down by thirteen points. They didn't give up, however. Instead, they changed their offensive attack plan and, ramped up by the crowd's chants of *Let's go Knicks*," surged from behind to win, 107–100.

"The fifth game was one of the greatest basketball games ever played," said Dave DeBusschere years later.

The Knicks couldn't pull it together for game six, however. Without Reed standing in his way, Wilt

Chamberlain was unstoppable, scoring 45 points in the 135–113 Laker victory.

The final and deciding game of the 1970 NBA Finals was played in Madison Square Garden. Nearly 20,000 hometown spectators showed up to watch the match. Before the game, everyone looked around the arena, hoping for a glimpse of Reed. But he was nowhere to be seen.

Then, moments before the start of the game, the Knicks' locker room door opened. A lone figure limped through the tunnel leading to the arena.

"Here comes Willis!" cried the announcer.

The crowd burst into applause and cheers. The noise only grew louder as Reed, looking shaky but determined, hobbled onto the floor to take a few warm-up shots.

As he did, teammate Dave DeBusschere glanced over at the Lakers. To a man, they were all staring at Reed. "At that point," he remembered later, "I thought they were defeated."

Reed hobbled to the center circle for the tip-off. It was obvious he was hurting, especially when he let Chamberlain jump for the ball uncontested. Some players might have decided then to leave the game.

Not Reed. He not only stayed in, he made the Knicks' first basket a mere eighteen seconds into the game! And then, less than a minute later, he drained basket number two.

Those were the only points Reed made that night. But his contribution to the game was far, far greater than any stat. His mere presence on the court inspired the Knicks to push themselves ever harder to win.

New York racked up the points, crashed the boards, and dogged Chamberlain, West, and Baylor. In the end, the Lakers scored just 99 points. The Knicks had 113 — and their first NBA championship title! Reed was named the Most Valuable Player, the third time that season he had been so honored (he was also the MVP of the All-Star Game and the league MVP).

"[Reed] gave us a tremendous lift, just going out there," Coach Holzman told reporters after the game.

"If Willis didn't do what he did, I wouldn't have been able to have the game I had," agreed Frazier, who had 36 points and 19 assists for the night. "He got the fans involved and gave us confidence just by his coming onto the floor."

Sometimes, it's great shooting or great defense that wins games. This time, it was the heart and soul of one man that inspired a team to victory.

The New York Knicks and the Los Angeles Lakers have met just two other times in the Finals. The Lakers nabbed the title in 1972, beating the Knicks four games to one. But the Knicks returned the favor the following year and bested Los Angeles by the same four-to-one margin. In the end, however, the Lakers have proved to be the better of the two teams. The Knicks have gone to the Finals eight times and won twice. The Lakers have been in the Finals thirty times and come away with fourteen championship titles.

★ JUNE 4, 1976 ★

CELTICS VERSUS SUNS

The Three-OT Final

The big news at the end of the 1976 NBA season was the rise of the Phoenix Suns. After coming in fourth place in the Pacific Division of the Western Conference for the last two seasons, the team jumped up a notch to third place, good enough to get them into the playoffs for the first time since 1970. They then fought their way past the Seattle Sonics and the Golden State Warriors to reach the Finals.

There they met the Boston Celtics, at that time the best team in NBA history, with twelve championship titles since 1949. The Celtics were once more the top-ranked team in the Eastern Conference with a record of 54 wins and 28 losses. Their roster included basketball veterans Dave Cowens, John Havlicek, Paul Silas, Jo Jo White, and Charlie Scott. Their coach was former player and Celtic great Tom Heinsohn.

The Suns' roster, by comparison, had just one star player, Paul Westphal, who had recently been traded to Phoenix by Boston. Overall, the Suns were a young team, existing only eight years as a franchise; coached by a man not much older than the players, John MacLeod; and featuring a twenty-one-year-old center-forward, Alvan Adams, in the starting lineup.

But what the Suns lacked in experience, they made up for in energy and ingenuity. The Celtics, meanwhile, called upon their tradition of superior defense and sharpshooting offense — while quietly acknowledging that some of their players were getting on in years and others were suffering from nagging injuries.

Despite this, most basketball followers predicted the Celtics would overpower the Suns easily, perhaps even sweep them from the Finals in four games. Not only had the Celtics put together a better overall season than the Suns, but the Suns hadn't beaten the Celtics since 1974!

At first, it seemed the predictions would come true. Boston won the first two games by double-digit margins. But they got a surprise in game three, played in Phoenix, when the Suns toppled them

43

105–98. They were showed up again in game four, when the Suns nabbed the win in the final minute, 109–107.

The series came back to Boston for game five. Cheering Celtics fans packed the stands, certain their team would go up in the game count that night.

But some of the Celtics themselves were not quite as sure. "We knew we were in a dogfight and we'd really have to lace them up to win," remembered Jo Jo White years later.

White and the other players, Celtics and Suns alike, had no way of knowing that this "dogfight" would end up being the longest Finals game ever played — although, at first, no one watching or playing would have thought that possible.

The first quarter was a lopsided affair that found the Celtics with twice as many points on the board as the Suns, 36–18, after the initial twelve minutes of play. Phoenix worked hard to make up the difference, but by the half, they still trailed by 16 points, 61–45.

It was a different story in the third quarter, however. The Suns clamped down on defense and held the Celtics to just 16 points. At the same time, they powered up their offense and closed the gap to a mere five points, 77–72.

The Suns continued to push hard in the fourth quarter, too. But the Celtics weren't about to give them the edge without a fight. With just a little more than a minute and a half remaining on the game clock, Boston still had a five-point lead. If they could just hold on for ninety seconds more, they would walk away with the win and go up in the series three games to two.

They couldn't hold on — or rather, they couldn't stop Paul Westphal. With the score 94–89 in favor of the Celtics, he tossed in a fadeaway jumper to make it 94–91. Then, when Boston tried to return the favor, he knocked the ball away from Jo Jo White. As Westphal took off like a rocket toward the other end of the court, Alvan Adams snared the ball and, with a mighty heave, threw it to Westphal. Westphal went up for the layup, made the shot, and was fouled. One free throw later, the score was tied, 94–94.

There was less than one minute remaining when Phoenix's Curtis Perry was fouled while shooting. He stepped to the foul line to take his two shots. He made one but missed the other. The Suns had a one-point lead.

Not for long. With the clock ticking down, the Celtics' John Havlicek was fouled. Now he had a chance to give Boston the game by making both free throws. But, like Perry, he hit only one. When the buzzer sounded, the score was still knotted, 95–95. The game would be decided in overtime.

But not the first overtime, as it turned out. In the five minutes that followed, both teams scored six points. Then, just as time was about to run out, Paul Silas signaled for a time-out.

There was just one problem: the Celtics didn't have any more time-outs! According to NBA rules, referee Richie Powers should have slapped Silas with a technical foul. That infraction would have given the Suns a single free throw, a shot that could very well have ended the game then and there.

But, for some reason, Powers didn't call the technical. Perhaps he didn't see Silas's signal. Or maybe he chose to ignore it. No one has ever determined the truth, and to this day, the matter remains one of the NBA's most controversial moments.

It was now closing in on midnight. Both teams were exhausted. Yet to determine the winner of the game, they would have to play another overtime period.

And what an overtime it ended up being! The teams traded baskets in the opening minutes, but with twenty seconds remaining, the Celtics took a three-point lead, 109–106.

Five seconds later, that lead was shaved to one point thanks to a sweet eighteen-foot jump shot by Dick Van Arsdale. The Celtics inbounded the ball from under the hoop — and had it stolen by Westphal! Westphal sent it to Perry.

Perry shot. . . . Missed!

Havlicek jumped for the rebound, only to have the ball plucked away by Perry, who shot again from sixteen feet away. And this time he made it! The lead had suddenly turned from 109–106 in the Celtics' favor to 110–109 for the Suns!

The Celtics had just six seconds left to perform a miracle. Forward Don Nelson took the ball out of bounds. He passed to Havlicek. Havlicek raced to his left with three powerful dribbles. Then he stopped and shot. The ball soared the fifteen feet to the basket and banked in! A moment later, the horn blared.

"The ball game is over! John Havlicek won it!" cried television announcer Brent Musburger.

The crowds surged onto the floor to mob their

favorite team. The Celtics rushed to the locker room to celebrate. Viewers at home were shown the final score: Boston 111, Phoenix 110.

But then something happened. Referee Powers called the teams back to the floor. Havlicek's shot had sunk with two seconds remaining on the clock. The game wasn't over until those last seconds were played.

The crowd on the floor was incensed. One fan even attacked Powers. But in due time the court was cleared, and the game resumed for the final seconds of play.

In a game full of controversy, last-ditch efforts, and gutsy play, those final seconds stand alone as two of the most remarkable ever played. First, Westphal did just what Silas had done earlier; that is, he called a time-out for the Suns knowing full well that Phoenix had none left.

This time, the referee called the technical foul. Jo Jo White went to the line. He bounced the ball, took a deep breath, and shot. Swish! The ball fell through! The Celtics were up 112–110!

But now the Suns had the ball at midcourt. With one final second still to be played, Perry prepared to inbound the ball.

"They'll have to throw it up," Brent Musburger cried excitedly just as Perry sent a pass to Garfield Heard. "Gar Heard turnaround shot in the air . . ." His call ended in a scream of amazement. "*Aahhhh!* It's good! It's tied again! I don't believe it!"

With that glory shot, known forever after as "the shot Heard 'round the world," game five of the Finals went into an unimaginable *third* overtime. Again, both sides fought hard with what little strength they had left. Again, the last seconds were electrifying. And again, it was Westphal who rallied his team and almost won the game for the Suns.

Almost.

This time, there would be no buzzer-beating shot or out-of-nowhere steal. There would be no miracle for Phoenix. When the game finally ended, the score stood at Boston 128, Phoenix 126.

Two nights later, Boston won their fourth game in the series to claim their thirteenth championship title. That last game had plenty of exciting moments. Yet in the end, game five was all anyone could talk about.

"It had so many heroes in it," Jo Jo White, the Finals MVP, commented years later. "So many players making so many big shots. It was draining. It was

49

strenuous. You had to reach down for everything you had to pull out a victory. It had all the dramatics that anyone could ask for."

Fittingly, that heroic, dramatic game has earned an equally heroic and dramatic title: the Greatest Game Ever Played.

The Boston Celtics claimed their place as the most dominant franchise in the history of the NBA with their 1976 championship victory. The next few years, however, the club declined, failing to even reach the playoffs in 1978 and 1979. Not until 1981 would they once again rise to the top, flying high on the wings of a player named Larry Bird.

★ MAY 11, 1980 ★

JULIUS ERVING

Dr. J's Baseline Move

When Julius Erving was in high school, he had a good friend he called "Professor." This friend had earned his nickname because he liked to talk on and on about whatever subject they were discussing — a habit that reminded Erving of a professor giving a lecture. The friend didn't mind the nickname but thought that Erving needed one, too. So he told Erving that if he was the Professor, then Erving must be the Doctor.

Erving's nickname eventually evolved into the one basketball followers know him by: Dr. J.

Dr. J arrived on the professional basketball scene in 1971, a chaotic time in the sport's history. Five years earlier, a new league, the American Basketball Association (ABA), had been created by businessmen hoping to establish lucrative franchises in places the NBA had not yet reached. Best known for its signature red, white, and blue basketball and its introduc-

51

tion of the three-point shot, the ABA promoted a flashy, acrobatic style of play — as well as flashy, acrobatic players.

Of all those players, none compared to Dr. J. A mediocre player who was not quite six feet tall as a freshman in high school, Erving grew tremendously in the years that followed. By the time he enrolled at the University of Massachusetts, he stood at nearly six feet seven inches tall. He had such enormous hands that a basketball held in his palm looked like an orange!

Erving had grown in skill as well as stature. Basketball scouts from both leagues watched him carefully. Then, in his junior year, the Virginia Squires of the ABA made him an offer. Erving accepted and left school to begin his professional career.

He made an immediate impact in the league. He could jump higher than the tallest player, hang in the air longer than seemed possible, and thread his way through the tightest defense. Every move he made was graceful, powerful, and controlled. While other players bulled to the basket and blindly stuffed the ball through the hoop, he floated above the rim, cradling the ball, and dunked it.

"When handling the ball," he recalled in an interview once, "I always would look for daylight. . . . Sometimes there's only a little bit of daylight between two players, and you'd find a way to get the ball between those two bodies and you make something happen."

Erving made something happen nearly every time he touched the ball. But he didn't just captivate people with his monstrous talent. He also impressed them with his dignified demeanor on and off the court. In a league where crazy antics and self-promotion were rampant, the Doctor kept his cool.

Erving played for the Squires for two seasons. Then, in 1973, he was traded to another ABA team, the New York Nets, where he played for another three years. Fans adored watching him play, but unfortunately, while he was soaring to ever greater heights with each passing year, the ABA was steadily losing ground to the NBA.

Unlike games in the NBA, ABA contests weren't shown on national television. Some games didn't even receive local coverage. That made it hard for the fledgling league to add to their already small fan base or to lure spectators away from the more easily accessible NBA. The ABA also had to battle the NBA for good players — and then, if they were lucky enough to get those players, they had to work hard to keep them. That became increasingly difficult as ticket sales dwindled and money grew tight.

Finally, in 1976, the ABA was left with two choices: fold completely or merge with the NBA. It chose to merge. The best players of the five lowest-ranking teams were cherry-picked for NBA teams. The remaining four teams — the Denver Nuggets, the New York Nets, the Indiana Pacers, and the San Antonio Spurs — became part of the NBA.

Erving was with the Nets at the time of the merger. The NBA and its fans were thrilled to have him in their league. In fact, some believe the NBA pushed for the merger for one simple reason: they wanted, perhaps even *needed,* Erving!

As it turned out, the NBA was not without its own troubles. Compared to the fast-action ABA games, NBA games were dull; compared to risk-taking ABA players, NBA players were cautious. Enthusiasm for the league, once so strong, had begun to fade.

All that changed in 1976. Before the start of the season, Erving was traded from the Nets to the Philadelphia 76ers. In no time at all, he charged the team with his special brand of energy, and dazzled players and fans alike with his gravity-defying moves and sharpshooting. Buoyed by Erving, the Sixers reached the Finals in 1977 for the first time in ten years. They were number one in the Atlantic Division again the following year, but made it only as far as the Eastern Conference finals. They made it farther in the playoffs in 1979 but lost to the San Antonio Spurs in the Eastern Conference semifinals.

It had to have been frustrating for Erving and the Sixers to have come so close to the championship three years in a row. Yet Erving rarely showed any dismay or anger. Instead, he remained as dignified as ever, proving to basketball followers everywhere that a person could be a fierce competitor without losing control.

"Julius was the first to truly take the torch and become the spokesman for the NBA," a former coach and longtime friend once said. "He understood what his role was and how important it was for him to conduct himself as a representative of the league."

The 1979–80 season found the Sixers falling just short of the Celtics to take the second-place slot again. But they roared through the playoffs, winning ten out of twelve games, including four against Boston, to reach the Finals for the second time since Erving joined the team. There they would face the

Los Angeles Lakers, a team loaded with incredible talent, including Kareem Abdul-Jabbar and rookie forward Earvin "Magic" Johnson.

The Lakers took the first game, 109–102. But the Sixers tied it up the next meeting, winning 107–104. Dr. J set the tone for that game by slamming down a dunk over Abdul-Jabbar in the first minutes. Unfortunately for Philadelphia, the Lakers stormed ahead three nights later, besting the Sixers 111–101, thanks in large part to the unstoppable Abdul-Jabbar, who scored 33 points and ripped down 14 rebounds.

Game four was also played in Philadelphia. The Spectrum Arena was packed with fans eager to see if their hometown heroes could knot the series at two games apiece. But that night, they got far more than they could have hoped for — they witnessed one of the greatest moves any basketball player has ever made.

The game was a hard-fought battle, and late in the fourth quarter, the score stood at 89–84 in favor of the Lakers. The Sixers got possession and fed the ball to Dr. J. He drove to the right baseline, beating defender Mark Landsberger as he did. Now he had a chance for a dunk or a layup. He leaped, ball palmed securely in his right hand, his left arm straight out to hold Landsberger at bay.

Suddenly, as Erving sailed above the baseline, Abdul-Jabbar jumped in front of him, arms high and ready to block the shot! In the blink of an eye, Dr. J shifted his trajectory — *in midair* — so that he sailed out of bounds with the ball an arm's length behind the backboard.

"So now here he is, walking through the air," said Magic Johnson, an on-the-floor eyewitness to the moment. "I'm thinking, 'There's no way Doc can float all the way from this side. We got him.'"

But they didn't have him. When Dr. J couldn't shoot from the right, he shot from the left — by swooping the ball under the hoop, past Abdul-Jabbar, and against the left side of the backboard for a reverse layup that gently banked through the net — *all while he was gliding through the air!*

The crowd exploded, roaring and cheering. The announcers bellowed in disbelief. Magic Johnson's jaw dropped open. "I could not believe my eyes because of the move this man had just made," he recalled later, his voice still full of amazement.

The Sixers won game four, 105–102, but in the

end, the Lakers won the Finals. The sixth game is nearly as memorable, for that's when rookie Magic Johnson stepped in for an injured Abdul-Jabbar and ended up with 42 points, 15 rebounds, 7 assists, and 3 steals. No doubt Magic was thrilled to have helped his team become the champions. Yet nothing compared to what he had witnessed Dr. J do two games earlier.

"It's still the greatest move I've ever seen in basketball," he once said. "The all-time greatest."

Julius "Dr. J" Erving played for the Philadelphia 76ers until 1987. When he was on the team, the Sixers went to the playoffs every year, and in 1983, they beat the Lakers to win the championship title. Erving retired with an ABA-NBA career total of 30,026 points, 10,525 rebounds, and 5,176 assists.

★ APRIL 5, 1984 ★

KAREEM ABDUL-JABBAR

The Record-Setting Hook

Picture Kareem Abdul-Jabbar taking a shot, and chances are, the shot imagined is his signature sky hook.

"Sometimes that beautiful sky hook . . . mmmmm," teammate Magic Johnson once rhapsodized, "that's the most beautiful shot that I've ever seen in basketball."

The shot's name was first coined by broadcaster Eddie Doucette in the mid-1970s, when Abdul-Jabbar was the star center for the Milwaukee Bucks. Doucette needed a way to describe the unusual shot.

"One night it just hit me," Doucette told the *New York Times*. "It's so different from anybody else's hook. It's not a flat hook, a baby hook, or a jump hook. It's a pure hook. And it does come out of the sky."

Abdul-Jabbar started using the sky hook early in life. "The first time I shot the hook, I was in fourth grade," he once said. "I was about five feet eight inches tall. I put the ball up and felt totally at ease with the shot."

His confidence in the sky hook never dwindled, and with good reason.

When done correctly, the shot is nearly impossible to block because the shooter's body is between the defender and the ball at all times. To set up for the shot, the shooter cradles the ball with both hands near his chin. Then he jumps up off his left foot and turns his left shoulder toward the hoop in midair. At the same time, he shifts the ball to his right hand and then swoops it up and over his head, aiming for the center of the rim. Finally, he flicks the ball with his fingers toward the hoop and *swish!* In it goes!

Not everyone can do the sky hook, but for those who can, it is a very powerful offensive tool. For Kareem, it wasn't just a tool — it was a devastating weapon, one that he unleashed with deadly accuracy thousands of times. At the buzzer, from the baseline, from the top of the key — Abdul-Jabbar stuck the sky hook so many times in the course of his twenty-year NBA career that it would be impossible to chronicle them all.

Yet there is one Abdul-Jabbar sky hook that outdid the rest. That shot came on April 5, 1984.

Abdul-Jabbar was the center for the Los Angeles Lakers by then, having been traded by the Milwaukee Bucks in 1975. He was nearly thirty-seven years old and had racked up an amazing list of achievements, including winning six Most Valuable Player awards and three NBA championship rings.

He had also racked up 31,398 regular-season points before that April 5 game — just 21 points shy of tying the all-time 31,419-point scoring record established by Wilt Chamberlain. Given that Abdul-Jabbar was averaging 21.5 points per game that season, there was no guarantee that he would meet or beat the record that night.

The Lakers were playing the Utah Jazz. The 18,000 fans who attended the game at the University of Nevada, Las Vegas knew what was on the line. Even though he was on the opposing team, Abdul-Jabbar received a standing ovation from the crowd that lasted a full forty-five seconds. He responded by waving and grinning broadly.

The Jazz were on their way to a first-place record

in the Midwest Division of the Western Conference that year, but that night they were no match for Kareem and the Lakers. Abdul-Jabbar may have been one of the oldest players on the court, but from the moment he hit the floor, he played with the passion and energy of a rookie. Years of training and a strict exercise regimen that included meditation, yoga, and martial arts had kept him flexible and strong — and strong was exactly how he started out. The first four times he got the ball, he made three dunks and a fadeaway jump shot!

Those four shots brought him 8 points closer to Chamberlain's record. As the game progressed, the announcer kept tabs on how many more he had to go. By the end of the first quarter, Abdul-Jabbar had chipped away 12 from the 21 he needed to tie. By halftime, he had added 4 more for a game total of 16. With an entire half still to play and only 5 more points needed to tie, 6 to break the record, it seemed inevitable that Kareem would nab the scoring crown that night.

Or would he? As the third quarter got under way, Abdul-Jabbar seemed more interested in helping his teammates score than scoring himself. Although he sank a sky hook to shrivel the points-needed total to three, he passed to open men and dished off a few assists instead of taking the ball to the hoop himself.

It wasn't until early in the fourth quarter that he seemed to decide to finish the job once and for all. He was fouled, stepped to the line, and sank a free throw.

Two left to tie the record, three to break it.

The tying shot came in a thunderous way. Teammate James Worthy got the ball and powered through the defense toward the hoop. Kareem was there, too. Worthy fed him the ball high in the air. Kareem leaped and slammed it through the basket!

The crowd went crazy. Kareem Abdul-Jabbar had just tied Wilt Chamberlain's record of 31,419 points! If he could get just one more basket, or even make just one more free throw, he would be the number one scorer in NBA history.

The points didn't come on his next possession. He shot, but it clanged off the rim.

The Jazz got the rebound and hurried to their end of the court for a shot. The ball bounced off the rim. Abdul-Jabbar leaped and swatted the rebound into the hands of Laker guard Magic Johnson. Johnson quickly dribbled downcourt. He handed off to Kareem near the top of the key. Kareem handed the ball back and moved to the low post. In the blink of an eye, Johnson flashed a pass to him.

Instantly, Utah's burly seven-feet-four-inch center, Mark Eaton, rushed to put himself between Abdul-Jabbar and the hoop. Guard Rickey Green pounced as well, reaching out to try and rip the ball from Kareem's hands.

Abdul-Jabbar reacted by faking a pass to teammate Michael Cooper. The defense followed his motion for just a split second — but that split second was all the veteran center needed.

"And the crowd is standing for Kareem. . . . Everybody is waving their arms," announcer Chick Hearn called, his voice tense with anticipation. "Kareem swings left, right-hand twelve-footer — GOOD!"

Whatever the announcer said next was drowned out by the roar of the fans. Kareem Abdul-Jabbar had just become the new NBA scoring king with a beautiful sky hook from twelve feet out on the right baseline!

The game stopped as Kareem and his parents were joined in the center circle of the court by NBA commissioner David Stern and throngs of cameramen and reporters. "You are one of the greatest athletes ever to play our game," Stern said in his speech, echoing the sentiments of everybody there.

Kareem accepted the game ball from Stern. Notoriously camera shy, he nevertheless took the microphone and, looking somewhat uncomfortable with all the attention, thanked his fans, teammates, and parents. But in the end, he didn't need to give a big speech. After all, as he pointed out, "It's hard to say anything when all is said and done."

Kareem Abdul-Jabbar retired from basketball in 1989 holding records in several categories including most points scored (38,387), most shots blocked (3,189), and most MVP awards given (6 NBA, 2 NBA Finals). The forty-two year old superstar owned six championship rings and had played in nineteen All-Star games. He had wowed fans, teammates, and rivals for twenty years, more seasons than any other player. Today he is a best-selling author and has starred in several movies, but it is for his signature sky hook that he will undoubtedly be remembered.

LARRY BIRD

The Steal

How big of an impact did Larry Bird make on the Boston Celtics? The records say it all: at the end of the 1978–79 NBA season, the year before Bird joined the team, the once-mighty Celtics were the worst team in the Atlantic Division with only 23 wins and 53 losses.

Then Larry Bird came to Boston — and the Celtics zoomed from worst to first with 61 wins and 21 losses, one of the greatest single-season reversals in NBA history.

How did the lanky forward from rural Indiana do it? He was one of the most well-rounded players to come to the game in a long time, rivaled only perhaps by another rookie, Magic Johnson of the Lakers. Bird could shoot. He could pass. He could rebound. Pressure situations? No problem — Bird only got better when the heat was on. Ball bouncing out of bounds?

There was Bird, lunging across the floor to make the save.

"Anytime you have Bird on the floor, anything can happen," NBA great Clyde Drexler once said.

But perhaps what made "Larry Legend" so amazing was his uncanny ability to "read" the game. Like an accomplished chess player, Bird could anticipate how the play was going to unfold and then change it according to how *he* wanted it to go. That ability isn't something a player can be taught. He either has it or he doesn't. Opposing teams soon learned that Bird had it, by the truckload.

Thanks to Bird, the Celtics were once again the "big-time" team of the Eastern Conference. They returned to the playoffs his rookie year, making it through the first round before falling to the Philadelphia 76ers. The next year, the Celtics improved their record by one win, romped through the playoffs, and beat the Houston Rockets four games to two to take the NBA title for the first time since 1976.

The 1981 Finals saw Bird soaring for an average of 21.9 points, 14 rebounds, and 6.1 assists. But his greatest moment was undoubtedly in the fourth quarter of game one. He had the ball in the right-top corner of the key. Two dribbles later, he was outside the foul line. He stopped, took aim, and fired a jump shot from nineteen feet.

The moment the ball left his hands, Bird seemed to know that the shot was going to fall short. So while the defense and the offense clustered under the hoop for the rebound, he darted forward. Sure enough, the ball ricocheted off the rim and bounced high in the air, far out of anybody's reach — except Bird's. Still in motion, he leaped, nabbed the rebound with his right hand, and, as his body floated out of bounds, switched the ball to his left and delivered an underhand shot that swished through the net!

Coach Auerbach called the shot the greatest play he had ever seen, which, considering how many unbelievable plays he had seen in his years, was saying quite a lot!

The Celtics won the championship again in 1984 and 1986. Bird was named Finals MVP for each of those two titles. He was also the league's MVP in those years, as well as in 1985.

Besides sparking the Celtics to ever-greater heights, Bird contributed to the game in another way: he brought excitement back to basketball and, in doing so, brought fans back to the stands. When the Celtics returned to the playoffs again in the 1986–87 season, they played to arenas packed with people who agreed that the NBA was, as its new slogan claimed, "FAN-tastic."

Several thousand of those fans were sitting in the stands of the Boston Garden for game five of the 1987 Eastern Conference finals. The Boston Celtics were battling the Detroit Pistons that night for the right to advance to the championship series.

Going into the fifth match, the series score was tied at two games apiece. The Pistons had the mental edge, however, having trounced the Celtics, 145–119, in their most recent meeting. Winning game five would increase their psychological advantage — a big step toward their goal of unseating the reigning titleholders.

Of course, Boston wasn't about to let that happen. Unlike in the previous match, they gave as good as they got throughout and, by the end of the fourth quarter, had racked up nearly as many points as Detroit.

Nearly. With less than ten seconds left on the game clock, the Pistons were ahead, 107–106. Bird got the ball outside the three-point line, did a neat little stagger step that moved his defender out of position, and then drove to the hoop. He leaped, ball held high and on its way to the basket, when — *wham!* The ball was slapped away, and Bird hit the floor. He slid backward for several feet, and the ball bounced out of bounds.

Although the ball appeared to have been touched last by Detroit, the referees — to the Celtics' disbelief — called the play in the Pistons' favor. So with five seconds remaining, the Pistons' star player, Isiah Thomas, took the ball out of bounds.

Boston set up on defense. Bird guarded his man at the top of the key. But at the same time, he watched Thomas — very, very closely. That's how he saw Thomas glance at fellow Piston Bill Laimbeer.

In a flash, Bird guessed what that glance meant. Thomas was going to pass to Laimbeer!

Sure enough, Laimbeer cut to the hoop. He was wide open when Thomas threw the ball over his Boston defender.

All of a sudden — *voom!* Bird flew from the top of the key and snared the ball just before it hit Laimbeer's outstretched hands! Bird zipped a pass to teammate Dennis "D. J." Johnson, who had moved underneath their basket. Johnson nabbed the ball under the hoop, turned, and laid it in for two points!

It had all happened so quickly that it took fans a moment to register what had happened. Then announcer Johnny Most spelled it out for them.

"What a play by Bird! Bird stole the inbounding pass!" Most shouted. His voice rose, raspy and frenzied, with each word. "Boston has a one-point lead with one second left! *Oh my! This place is going crazy!*"

Bird's steal and D. J.'s shot sealed the win for the Celtics. Boston went on to beat Detroit the next outing to advance to the Finals. Unfortunately, that was the end of the road for the Celtics, who lost the championship to Magic Johnson and the Los Angeles Lakers. But their journey would have been much shorter had it not been for Bird's uncanny ability to read the game.

Larry Bird spent his entire thirteen-year career with the Boston Celtics. After participating in the 1992 Summer Olympics as a member of the original Dream Team, he retired because of nagging back problems. Bird is considered one of the greatest all-around players in NBA history.

★ JUNE 9, 1987 ★

MAGIC JOHNSON

The Junior, Junior Sky Hook

Earvin "Magic" Johnson jumped into the hearts of millions the first time he took to the court in a Los Angeles Lakers uniform. It was the team's 1979 season opener. The Lakers were playing the San Diego Clippers in a match that went down to the wire. As the final seconds ticked off, Kareem Abdul-Jabbar stuck his signature sky hook to give the Lakers a 103–102 victory.

A buzzer-beating win was a nice way for the Lakers to begin their season, of course. But Magic, who got his nickname in high school after dazzling the local media with his acrobatic style of play, treated the victory as if it were game seven of the Finals. He charged across the floor, threw his arms around Abdul-Jabbar, and hugged him, all the while beaming his 100-watt smile.

Johnson's enthusiasm for basketball never dwindled. Each season found him doing something amaz-

The famous Wilt Chamberlain "100" photo, taken in the locker room on March 2, 1962, after the center made history as the only NBA player to score one hundred points in regulation time.

On May 14, 1980, Julius Erving, aka Dr. J, seems to walk on air on his way to the hoop.

Kareem Abdul-Jabbar goes up with his signature, nearly-impossible-to-block shot, the sky hook. On April 5, 1984, he became the highest scorer in NBA history, surpassing Wilt Chamberlain's record by hitting his 31,420th point with—what else?—the sky hook!

Earvin "Magic" Johnson is magic under the basket, punching the ball away from the Celtics in the 1987 NBA Finals. He would later save the game with a shot he dubbed the "junior, junior sky hook."

The Shot: A split second before the final horn sounds to end Game 5 of the 1989 Eastern Conference Finals, Michael Jordan goes up for a jump shot—and makes it! Bulls win!

Larry Bird celebrates moments after his amazing game-winning steal in the 1987 Eastern Conference Finals.

Kobe Bryant, the NBA's Most Valuable Player in 2008, drains two of an unbelievable eighty-one points in a game on January 22, 2006.

Old school meets new school: Bill Russell and Kevin Garnett—two Celtics greats—celebrate Boston's seventheeth World Championship in 2008.

ing on the court. In the 1980 NBA Finals, the six-foot-nine-inch guard stepped in at center for an injured Kareem Abdul-Jabbar and proceeded to score 42 points, pull down 15 rebounds, pass for 7 assists, and chalk up 3 steals!

His behind-the-back passes astonished even his teammates. "There have been times when he has thrown passes and I wasn't sure where he was going," Laker Michael Cooper once said. "Then one of our guys catches the ball and scores, and I run back up the floor convinced that he must've thrown it through somebody."

When negative publicity rained down on him early in his career — he was blamed for coach Paul Westhead being replaced by Pat Riley and derided when his play faltered — Johnson didn't fire back or bury his head in the sand. He refused to give up when he stumbled, for the simple reason that he loved to play basketball.

In fact, rather than throwing in the towel, Magic did something some celebrity players don't do: he worked hard to improve his game. He was an impressive all-around player, routinely racking up triple-double stats, but sometimes his shooting left something to be desired. In game three of the first round of the 1981 playoffs against the Houston Rockets, for example, he launched a last-second shot that might have won the game for the Lakers. But instead of swishing neatly through the net, the shot was a disappointing air ball.

So Magic worked to improve his shot from all spots on the floor. He also practiced different types of shots, including one he hoped to master, the sky hook. And as luck would have it, he was a teammate of the undisputed master of that shot, Kareem Abdul-Jabbar.

"Earvin got to post up a lot of smaller guards," Abdul-Jabbar recalled, "and it was the perfect shot for him to use. So I worked with him to get his mechanics right."

Under Kareem's tutelage, Magic practiced the sky hook over and over throughout the 1986–87 season. His determination to get that shot and others just right paid off handsomely. He had some of the highest-scoring games of his career that year, and ended the season with a career-best average of 23.9 points per game. He also averaged 12.2 assists and 6.3 rebounds.

The Lakers steamrolled to the number one slot in the Pacific Division, and then flattened their opponents in the first three playoff rounds to advance to the Finals. There they met the Boston Celtics. Since 1959, when the Lakers were still in Minneapolis, these two teams had faced off in the Finals nine times. Eight of those times, the Celtics had emerged victorious. Only in their last matchup, in 1985, had the Lakers managed to beat the Boston team.

To say Los Angeles wanted a win this time around is putting it mildly. And they believed they had a very good chance of winning, for the Celtics had been plagued by injuries all year. Boston had literally limped its way through the playoffs, finally making it to the Finals after seventeen hard-fought games.

The Lakers, on the other hand, had needed only twelve games to reach the championship round. Compared to the exhausted Celtics, they were fresh and ready to go. They took the first two games easily by double-digit margins, thanks in large part to incredible performances by Magic Johnson. He posted 29 points, 13 assists, and 8 rebounds in game one, and 22 points and 20 assists in game two.

The Celtics scrambled to stay alive in game three, finally eking out a 109–103 win due to strong play from their bench. Buoyed by that victory, they thundered through the first half of game four. Going into the third quarter, they were ahead by 16 points.

The Lakers powered back, however, shaving that lead to eight with less than four minutes remaining in the game. Then, slowly but surely, they inched closer until, with thirty seconds left, they were behind by just a single point.

What happened in those last thirty seconds was a championship finale that may go down as one of the most memorable ever. First, Kareem Abdul-Jabbar scored on an alley-oop to give the Lakers a one-point lead. But Larry Bird of the Celtics answered with a beautiful three-pointer that stole the lead right back.

The Lakers took the ball out from under the hoop with twelve seconds left in the game. They raced to the opposite end of the court and fed the ball to Abdul-Jabbar. Kareem went up for a shot and was fouled. He made the first free throw to bring the score to 106–105 in Boston's favor. But he missed the tying shot.

The Celtics' star forward, Kevin McHale, nabbed the rebound — only to have Mychal Thompson of the Lakers whack it out of his hands and out of bounds. The referees called the play for the Lakers, despite protests from the Boston bench.

The inbound pass came to Magic near the left of the key. He turned to shoot a twenty-foot jumper. McHale leaped out to stop him, so Magic faked the shot instead, put the ball to the floor, and dribbled toward the hoop.

McHale was right with him. So were Bird and the Celtics' center, Robert Parish. In a tight three-on-one situation with the clock ticking down and the game on the line, Johnson stopped short, turned his left shoulder to the basket, and arced the ball toward the hoop with his right hand. Sky hook!

The ball floated just above Parish's fingertips, kissed the glass, and dropped in. Two seconds later, the buzzer sounded. After trailing for most of the game, the Lakers had won, 107–106!

"You expect to lose on a sky hook," Larry Bird said afterward, a rueful smile on his face. "You don't expect it to be from Magic."

After the game, Magic laughingly called the winning shot his "junior, junior sky hook," and that famous shot has been known by that name ever since.

The Lakers went on to win the 1987 Finals, 4–2. Magic played outstanding ball throughout and for his efforts was named the Finals MVP — his third time receiving that honor. Five years and three league MVPs later, he shocked the basketball world by announcing that he was retiring. He then revealed that he had contracted HIV, the virus that causes AIDS. Luckily for his fans, Magic returned to basketball to play in the 1992 Olympics.

★ MAY 7, 1989 ★

MICHAEL JORDAN

The Shot

Michael Jordan. His name is synonymous with basketball superstardom. He is arguably the greatest of the greats and unquestionably the best-known athlete in the world. He has inspired countless young basketball hopefuls to work their hardest to achieve their dreams.

A highlight reel of Jordan's best shots usually includes monstrous dunks, gravity-defying jumpers, and buzzer-beating baskets. But of all these, one stands out as the cream of the crop. That one is called, simply, "The Shot."

Jordan had had plenty of outstanding moments and hit plenty of milestones prior to The Shot. In the 1986 postseason, he scored 63 points in a heartbreaking double-overtime loss to the Boston Celtics. Those points marked a new postseason record that has yet to be broken. The following year, he became the second player after Wilt Chamberlain to score

3,000 points in a single regular season and the first to make 200 steals and 100 blocks. He dunked his way into the hearts of millions at the 1988 Slam Dunk Contest with a double-clutch throw down that started at the free throw line and saw him airborne all the way to the hoop.

"His Airness," as Jordan was often called, was such an overwhelming offensive force that in 1988 the Detroit Pistons devised a defense aimed at stopping him. The "Jordan Rules," as they were known, called for the Pistons to double- and triple-team him, to play him physically, and to keep the ball out of his hands at all costs.

"He could hurt you equally from either wing," recalled Detroit's coach Chuck Daly, who originated the Jordan Rules. "[Heck], he could hurt you from the hot dog stand!"

. But try as the Pistons and the other teams might, they couldn't shut down Jordan. He outscored every other player in the league for the second year in a row during the 1988–89 season, with an average of 32.5 points per game. His efforts helped the Bulls make it into the postseason for the fifth consecutive time.

The Chicago Bulls faced the Cleveland Cavaliers

in the first round of the playoffs. The Bulls had beaten the Cavs the previous year, 3–2, and were hopeful of repeating or bettering that performance.

Naturally, Cleveland was just as eager to come out on top. They had reason to believe they would, as they had won ten more games in the regular season than the Bulls had, and in the one meeting between the two teams five days earlier, Cleveland had emerged victorious, 90–84.

The Cavs had one other factor weighing in their favor: so far, Michael Jordan and the Bulls had failed to reach the Finals. Often, in fact, they had fallen in the first round of the playoffs. That trend had detractors claiming that Jordan simply didn't have what it took to boost his team to the very top.

The two teams met for game one on April 25, 1989. The Bulls emerged victorious with a score of 95–88. But the Cavs knotted the series two nights later with a nearly identical score of 96–88. Chicago knocked off another win in game three, 101–94, but once again Cleveland evened things up with a dramatic 108–105 overtime win in game four. The series would be decided in the fifth and final game.

Game five was played in Cleveland before an adoring and roaring crowd of more than twenty thousand fans. Those roars grew louder with each passing minute of the game, as the Cavaliers held the lead right up to the remaining seconds of the fourth quarter. Then, with just six seconds on the clock, Jordan made a jump shot that put the Bulls ahead for the first time.

The score was 99–98. The Cavaliers' Craig Ehlo inbounded the ball and quickly got a return pass. He put the ball on the floor and drove to the hoop for a layup. With less than four seconds left, the score was now 100–99!

What happened next has been recognized, time and again, as the most legendary shot in basketball history. It began with straightforward instructions from the Bulls' coach, Doug Collins.

"Give the ball to Michael," he told his team, "and everyone else get out of the way."

That's exactly what the Bulls did. With the crowd chanting, "Defense! Defense!" Brad Sellers took the ball out from the sidelines. He hit Jordan with a pass. Michael took two dribbles and then stopped short at the foul line. Craig Ehlo was right on top of him. Both men jumped at the same time, Jordan aiming the ball at the hoop, Ehlo aiming his hand at the ball.

Jordan soared into the air — and just seemed to keep going higher and higher. Finally, he released the ball. Ehlo stretched as far as he could, but there was just no way he could reach the ball. It brushed past his fingertips and floated up, over to the basket, and then in!

"Jordan . . . scores at the buzzer!" announcer Dick Stockton cried. "Michael Jordan has won it for Chicago! Michael Jordan hit the basket at the buzzer!"

He had indeed, and not just with that miraculous shot. Jordan had 44 total points, plus 9 rebounds and 6 assists, in the unbelievable 101–100 win. In an interview immediately after The Shot, Jordan was clearly happy but just as obviously exhausted. Still, he complimented his teammates on their performances, and then wrapped it all up by saying, "We won. And that's all that counts."

After beating the Cleveland Cavaliers in the first round of the 1989 playoffs, the Chicago Bulls bested the New York Knicks to advance to the Eastern Conference Finals. Unfortunately, that's as far as they got that year. The Detroit Pistons, the eventual NBA champions, defeated Michael Jordan and his teammates in the series, 4–2.

★ JUNE 5, 1991 ★

MICHAEL JORDAN

The Move

At the end of the 1990–91 regular season, Michael Jordan and the Chicago Bulls had one thing on their minds: winning their first NBA Finals. They had reached the playoffs every year since Jordan had joined the team in 1984, but never had they advanced farther than the Eastern Conference Finals. This year, the title was in their sights, and they were ready to charge forward and claim it.

The Bulls finished their schedule with 61 wins and 21 losses, the best in the Central Division and second best in the league after the powerful Portland Trail Blazers. In the postseason, they swept the New York Knicks in three lopsided games and then dispatched the Philadelphia 76ers in round two to advance to the Eastern Conference Finals.

There they faced the reigning champs, the Detroit Pistons. The Pistons had bounced the Bulls out of contention the previous year by winning game seven of the Eastern Conference Finals by nearly 20 points. Chicago fans held their collective breath now, wondering if the "Bad Boys" of Detroit would once again target their defense on Jordan and ride roughshod over their team in general.

They needn't have worried. With Michael Jordan spearheading the attack, the Bulls flattened the Pistons in four straight games. The final match saw Chicago winning by 21 points, 115–94. Jordan had posted 29 points, proving once again that even when he was double- and triple-teamed, he could find a way to put the ball through the hoop.

Having sent the Pistons home to lick their wounds, the Bulls now readied themselves for their final challenge: the Los Angeles Lakers. The Lakers had been one of the strongest teams for years. Since the 1979–80 season, they had made eight trips to the NBA championship. Five of those trips had ended in victory. Led by the versatile Magic Johnson, the Lakers not only had the talent to win again, they had the experience of playing in the league's most stressful series.

But the Bulls had something the Lakers didn't have: Michael Jordan. And this year, Jordan wanted nothing more than to silence his critics — those people who claimed that, as good as he was, he didn't have the stuff to win the championship.

The two teams met in Chicago on June 2, 1991, for game one. And what a game it was! Fans were kept on the edges of their seats until the very end. With half a minute to play, the Bulls were up by two points. If they could just hold on to their lead for thirty seconds, they could put the win in their pockets. Even if they gave up a single two-point basket, they could still pull out a victory in overtime. Right?

Wrong. Unbelievably, first Magic Johnson and then Sam Perkins hit shots that gave the Lakers a two-point lead.

But all was not lost! As the final seconds ticked off the clock, Michael Jordan got the ball. He dribbled, faked to the right, moved left, stopped on a dime, and jumped high to shoot over the desperate defender. The ball soared, arcing toward the basket. It touched the rim, bounced around, and then . . . bounced out! The game-tying shot had missed! That night, it would be the city of Los Angeles that would celebrate, not Chicago.

But the game one victory was just that — one victory. Three nights later, the Bulls arrived at Chicago Stadium ready to even the series at one game apiece.

Jordan, however, seemed to be looking for even more. He was, as announcer Bob Costas put it, "hoping for a second chance to send the stadium fans into basketball ecstasy."

Former Laker coach Pat Riley had one piece of advice for the Bulls: "Just do what you do a little bit better."

Unfortunately for Bulls fans, it didn't seem at first that Jordan would do what he did — make baskets — any better at all. In fact, in the first twenty minutes of the game, he did a whole lot worse, scoring only two points! While winning is a team effort, not a one-man show, Jordan typically set the pace for the Bulls. If his shooting hand didn't turn hot soon, Chicago would likely face another home-court loss.

And if they did lose, history was not on their side: no team had ever won the Finals after losing the first two games on their own court.

Perhaps Michael knew that. Or perhaps he just found his rhythm. Either way, he started hitting his shots, one after another — suddenly, he couldn't miss.

Meanwhile, Jordan's teammates were hitting with just as much success. Horace Grant chalked up 14 first-half points. John Paxson, unbelievably, didn't miss a single shot all night! The Bulls held a close

5-point lead at halftime and then surged ahead in the third quarter, adding 38 points to their side to go up 86–69.

Chicago fans were stomping, cheering, and roaring with glee. Here was the team that had excited them all season! And there was Jordan, their favorite player, sticking it to the Lakers time and again!

By the middle of the fourth quarter, a Chicago win seemed inevitable. With eight minutes left to play, the Bulls were up 95–71. Los Angeles' forward A. C. Green tried to make it 95–73, but his shot clanged off the rim.

Jordan got his hands on the ball and dribbled it down the court. At the top of the three-point line, he dished to Cliff Levingston at the front-left corner of the key. Levingston put the ball to the floor and took two steps toward the hoop. He jumped as if to shoot.

At the same moment, Jordan cut straight into the paint. Levingston twisted in midair and rifled a pass directly into Michael's waiting hands. Jordan drove toward the hoop.

Laker Byron Scott moved to intercept. Jordan brushed past him as if he didn't exist. He leaped from a point near the free throw line. He held the ball high over his head in his right palm, ready to thrust it through the hoop for a dunk.

Suddenly, Sam Perkins of the Lakers darted toward him. Perkins seemed determined to keep that dunk, or even a simple layup, from happening. Had he tried to stop any other player, he probably would have succeeded.

But Jordan was not any other player. The path to the right-handed dunk blocked? No sweat! He lowered the ball, switched it to his left hand, and calmly flipped it into the hoop from the left. A simple layup? Not quite! Jordan had made the switch and the shot *in midflight*!

"Oh! A spectacular move by Jordan!" the announcer screamed. "That's thirteen consecutive field goals!"

Jordan pumped his fist and then threw his arms around Levingston. Coach Phil Jackson broke into a huge grin. Teammate Scott Williams flung his arms wide and spun around, urging the crowd to celebrate the wondrous move with him. The announcers quickly checked the stat records to see if Jordan's 13-for-13 streak was the best ever in playoff history.

It wasn't, but in the end, no one really cared because the shot itself had been so impressive.

The day after the game, a 107–86 blowout, Jordan met with the press. Naturally, they all wanted to know what had gone through his head just before he made "The Move," as they were calling it.

"I probably had a wide-open shot, didn't I?" Michael replied with an impish grin. "I probably didn't even need to do that stuff at the end, huh?" He grinned more broadly and added, "You know what? It wasn't even one of my best creative shots."

Michael Jordan played thirteen seasons with the Chicago Bulls, leading the team to three consecutive championship titles from 1991–93. He shocked the world when he suddenly announced his retirement in 1993, saying that he intended to move to a new game — baseball. After a short stint with Chicago's minor-league team, he returned to the Bulls in 1995 with a simple statement: "I'm back." He retired again in 1999 after helping the Bulls to their second "three-peat": three consecutive championship titles.

★ FEBRUARY 1, 1995 ★

JOHN STOCKTON

King of Assists

John Stockton of the Utah Jazz was never interested in being in the spotlight. In fact, he downright avoided it whenever he could. And when he couldn't, he deflected the attention away from himself and onto his teammates.

But on February 1, 1995, he had no choice but to let the light shine directly on him. That's because he was on the verge of breaking an NBA record, the greatest number of career assists, which was held by one of the league's most beloved players, Magic Johnson.

When the game began, Stockton took the floor with the other starters, including the player with whom his name will be forever linked: Karl Malone. Malone was a power forward who had joined the Jazz one year after Stockton. Despite their differences in personality and style of play — Stockton was reserved while Malone was outspoken; Malone

91

was showy while Stockton kept a low profile — the two clicked on the court almost from the start.

After teaming up, they soon became one of the hottest basketball duos ever to play in the NBA. They worked one particular offensive maneuver, the classic pick-and-roll, so well together that the phrase "Stockton-to-Malone" has become synonymous with that play.

But when announcers bellowed, "Stockton-to-Malone!" it meant something else as well. Stockton seemed to have a sixth sense for where Malone would move. Drawing on that instinct, he hit Malone night after night with perfectly timed passes. And because Malone was just as tuned into Stockton, he would usually be ready to catch that pass — and to turn it into an assist by putting the ball right through the hoop. With every Stockton-to-Malone play, Malone's career point total increased by two and Stockton's assist total went up by one.

Malone wasn't the only player on the receiving end of Stockton's passes, of course. In fact, Stockton connected with all his teammates for shots time after time, season after season. While their point totals mounted, his assist number rose to greater heights. By 1986, he had 1,000 career assists; by 1990, he was up to 5,000. On February 17, 1992, he passed the legendary Celtic guard Bob Cousy by posting his 6,956th assist. Three years later, on January 28, 1995, he vaulted into the second-place slot when he bested the great Oscar Robertson's long-standing record of 9,887 assists.

Now only Magic Johnson had more assists to his credit than John Stockton. Johnson left the game in 1991 with 9,921 in that stat column. Going into the February 1 game against the Denver Nuggets, Stockton needed 10 to tie and 11 to beat that record. Since he was averaging 12 assists per game, it seemed inevitable that he would take over the first-place slot without a problem.

But would it be that night? And if so, who would catch his historic pass and make the shot?

The Jazz and the Nuggets were playing in Utah before a sellout crowd of nearly twenty thousand fans. In the stands hung a huge sign with an 11 on it — the number of assists Stockton needed to beat Magic's record. Each time he dished for a successful score that night, the number on the banner would change, in the style of a flip chart, to show how many assists remained. Every fan in the crowd hoped that before the game's end that number would be zero.

Stockton undoubtedly hoped so, too. But at the same time, he was worried that his record-breaking run might cause problems on the court.

"I'd feel terrible if everyone's concentration was on assists — my passing it to them, and them taking shots quickly, trying to get this record," he said just before the game. "And if we would lose the game, that would really taint it."

He needn't have been concerned. That night, the Jazz leaped to an early 25–4 lead over the struggling Nuggets. In that time, Stockton handed off five assists and scored a basket of his own within six consecutive possessions.

The number on the banner was flipping so quickly that by the middle of the second quarter, it had dropped to one. Stockton had tied Magic's record and now needed just a single assist to break it!

Suddenly, tension mounted in the arena. No one doubted Stockton would surpass Magic that night. But for his record-breaking moment to be truly memorable, there could be only one player on the receiving end of his pass. That player was Karl Malone — and he was sitting on the bench!

Malone wanted his friend's historic pass to be a classic Stockton-to-Malone as much as anyone else did. His teammates agreed, and luckily, so did his coach. With less than seven minutes remaining in the second quarter, he ordered Malone to go into the game.

Malone checked in and joined his teammates. The Jazz had possession. Stockton brought the ball across center court. Malone posted up to the left of the key. Stockton stopped and bounced a high pass to him. Malone caught the ball, turned away from his defender, and shot. The ball arced up and fell through the net, making the laces dance!

Assist number 11! Stockton had the record!

The crowd leaped to its feet, erupting into cheers. The game stopped so that Stockton could acknowledge the applause. But true to his nature, he didn't celebrate for long. After all, there was still a game to be won, and in John Stockton's book, that was more important than his record.

After the game, which the Jazz did win commandingly, 129–88, Stockton took a few minutes to talk to the press. But as was typical, he turned the conversation away from himself by praising others.

"My teammates were going to make sure the record happened," he said. "There were just some unbelievable shots that I won't soon forget."

He added that he was especially pleased Malone was the one who made the shot that turned his pass into a record-breaking assist. "He's been responsible for so many of them, it does seem fitting."

And how did Magic Johnson feel about having his record broken? He seemed positively delighted when he appeared on the JumboTron to congratulate Stockton. "John, from one assist man to another, you are the greatest team leader I have ever played against," he said, beaming.

John Stockton played his entire nineteen-year career with the Utah Jazz. On December 5, 2000, nearly five years after beating Magic's assist record, he helped Karl Malone surpass Wilt Chamberlain as the second-highest scorer in NBA history with a routine Stockton-to-Malone play. Stockton retired in 2003 with an astonishing, and possibly unbeatable, record of 15,806 assists.

☆ JUNE 5, 2000 ☆

SHAQUILLE O'NEAL

Rally-Oop!

Of all the big men currently in the NBA, few have as good a sense of humor as does Shaquille O'Neal. Whether poking fun at himself or other players, bantering with the press, or entertaining children in need by dressing up as "Shaq-a-Claus" at Christmas, O'Neal has managed to keep fans smiling since his rookie year.

But when he's on the court, he's all business — and his business is winning games and taking teams to the Finals.

Shaq was drafted by the Orlando Magic in 1992 and made an instant impact on the four-year-old team. At seven feet one and weighing more than three hundred pounds, he was a force to be reckoned with and capable of snatching rebounds over the heads of smaller players, driving the lane on the way to layups, and most thrilling of all, laying down thunderous dunks. His dunks were so thunderous, in fact, that twice during his rookie season he pulled the entire hoop structure down with him!

He helped the Magic win twenty more games in the 1992–93 season than they had won the previous year. By 1994–95, he had driven them all the way to the Finals. Unfortunately for Orlando fans, their team was swept by the more-seasoned Houston Rockets that year. These same fans received another blow the next season when they learned that their star center was leaving the Magic to join the Los Angeles Lakers.

O'Neal's combination of sheer power and surprising quickness boosted the 1996–97 Lakers to their best record since 1991. He and his teammates quickly dispatched the Portland Trail Blazers in the first round of the playoffs, only to fall to the Utah Jazz in the semifinals.

The Lakers improved their record the next year and once more made it to the playoffs — only to lose to the Jazz again in the semifinals. The 1998–99 season was a blip on the basketball radar screen — for due to a dispute between the NBA and the players, the first games weren't played until February! Still, in the shortened fifty-game schedule, the Lakers emerged with thirty-one wins. Shaq was again a big reason for the team's success, although a second member of the squad was emerging as an equally important cog in the Lakers' victory machine.

Kobe Bryant had first made headlines in 1996 when he was drafted into the NBA straight out of high school. Bryant spent his first two seasons coming off the Lakers' bench. But by 1998, his massive talent had earned him a spot in the starting lineup — and he never looked back. By the 1999–2000 season, he was regularly scoring in double digits, as well as nabbing rebounds and dishing assists in numbers nearly as high. On court, he and Shaq formed a one-two punch that few teams could match.

The Lakers roared into the 2000 postseason, winning an amazing 67 out of 82 games, the best in their division. Shaq led the league in points per game with 29.7; he also led the team in rebounds, with 13.6 per game. Kobe stepped up his play as well and wound up with 4.9 assists per game, the team's best.

O'Neal was now in his eighth year with the NBA. He had reached the playoffs in all but his first. But so far he had failed to win the coveted championship ring.

His determination to win one this time was clear in the first round against the Sacramento Kings. Shaq absolutely attacked the hoop, posting 46 points, 29 of which came in the second half alone! Those points cleared the way for the Lakers' 117–107 win.

But that was just one win. "We're on a mission here," O'Neal said shortly after the game. And that mission was to *keep winning*.

That's just what the Lakers did. They beat the Kings in four games in the best-of-five series to move to the semifinals. There they met — and beat — the Phoenix Suns. Next up were the Portland Trail Blazers.

The Trail Blazers entered the series with a very specific plan in mind. That plan was called the "Hack-a-Shaq," and it called for Portland's players to do exactly that: hack, or foul, Shaq. O'Neal was an inconsistent free throw shooter — "Me shooting forty percent at the foul line is just God's way to say nobody's perfect," he once said — and the Blazers figured they could keep his scoring down by putting him on the line. They also figured that a physical game that found Shaq double- and triple-teamed throughout would wear on the big man.

They figured wrong. Shaq hit 13 of 26 free throws in the first game, 12 of 25 in the fourth quarter alone. In all, he made 41 points and had 11 rebounds, 7 assists, and 5 blocked shots in the 109–94 win. "It hasn't worked all year," Shaq commented about the Blazers' inability to contain him, "and it ain't gonna work."

The Trail Blazers fought back the next match, however, and trounced the dumbfounded Lakers, 109–77. Kobe Bryant made a game-saving block in their third outing, preventing a possible overtime decision in the Lakers' 93–91 victory. Los Angeles took game four as well, 103–91. They needed just one more win to take the series and advance to the Finals.

They didn't get it the next match — or the one after that. Suddenly, the series was tied at three games apiece!

Shaq was undoubtedly frustrated by his team's apparent collapse, but he remained determined nonetheless. "We have to lay it all down," he said in an interview after game six. "The fans have to be ready, the city has to be ready, and the players have to be ready."

The seventh and final game of the series was played before nearly 20,000 cheering fans in Los Angeles. Those cheers grew quiet, however, as the Blazers slowly took the lead. At the end of the first quarter, Portland was up by seven. By halftime, their lead had shrunk to just three. But then, in the third quarter, they steamrolled ahead to an eleven-point advantage — an advantage that grew by four more points in the first minutes of the last quarter!

No team in the history of the NBA playoffs had ever before overcome such a huge deficit in game seven to win. For the Lakers to do just that seemed downright impossible.

But then something happened. With ten and a half minutes left on the clock, Shaq scored two points. Then he made a free throw. Teammate Brian Shaw drained a three-pointer. Kobe and Shaq both made points from the line. Robert Horry of the Lakers chalked up a three-pointer — and then Kobe posted two more points, followed by yet another three-pointer by Shaw!

The score was tied, 75–75! Fifteen unanswered points in six minutes! The Lakers were suddenly 100 percent back in the game, and they weren't done yet!

The Trail Blazers went up by two, only to see the score even up a second time when Shaq hit two from the foul line. Then it was Shaq again, sinking a hook shot to give the Lakers the lead with just over two minutes remaining.

Once more Portland tied it up, this time on a shot from Rasheed Wallace. But Los Angeles was not to be denied. Kobe was fouled and made both of his free throws to put the Lakers ahead by two. He hit a jump shot moments later, skying over veteran Scottie Pippen, to stretch the lead to four.

Then came the play of the game. With less than a minute remaining, Pippen tried for a three-pointer. His shot ricocheted off the rim. Shaq jumped up, caught the ball, and sent it to Kobe. Then as Kobe dribbled downcourt, Shaq jogged toward the far hoop.

The Trail Blazers had guarded O'Neal closely throughout the game — throughout the entire series, in fact. But this time, they took their eyes off him. It was just for a moment, but that moment was long enough for Shaq to make his move.

He cut to the basket, arm raised to signal Kobe. Kobe caught the signal. He dribbled quickly to the foul line, leaped, and lobbed a pass toward the hoop.

Shaq jumped with the pass. He snared the ball in his huge right hand and, with forty seconds showing on the game clock, slammed the ball through the basket for a resounding dunk!

The crowd went wild. Shaq raced to the other end of the court, waving his index fingers in the air and yelling right along with them. Players from the bench swarmed him before quickly returning to the sidelines.

Shaq's last-minute alley-oop punctuated the single greatest turnaround in NBA playoff history. When the final horn sounded, the Lakers had won, 89–84.

"My father once told me that even if you shoot ninety-nine percent and don't make the ones you're supposed to make, nothing else matters," O'Neal said after the game.

Fortunately for Lakers fans, Shaq made all the ones that mattered that night.

The Lakers won the NBA Finals that year, as well as in 2001 and 2002, joining the Minneapolis Lakers, the Boston Celtics, and the Chicago Bulls as one of the only teams in history to "three-peat" as champions. Shaq was awarded the Finals MVP each time, and in 2002 he once again led in scoring and re-

bounding. He played two more seasons with Los Angeles before moving back to Florida to play for the Miami Heat. Today he is a member of the Phoenix Suns. Kobe Bryant, meanwhile, has become the Lakers' star player. In 2008, he earned his first league MVP award in recognition of his outstanding team play.

★ MARCH 27, 2004 ★

LEBRON JAMES

Rookie Romp

On May 22, 2003, the city of Cleveland, Ohio, had its wildest basketball dream come true. That was when the NBA announced the picking order for its upcoming draft. The Cleveland Cavaliers were first on the list, and that meant one thing: they would get to choose LeBron James.

Eighteen-year-old James was a high school basketball phenom, a true superstar who could dribble, shoot, pass, and lead his team to victory after victory. Sure, he was young, but he wasn't the first teenager to go straight from high school to the NBA. Almost everyone who followed basketball believed that he would be the next great player in the league. *Sports Illustrated* had predicted just that when they put him on their cover the year before, along with the headline "The Chosen One."

Still, no one really knew for sure how James

would perform for the Cavaliers. Would the pressure be too much? Would he falter when going up against more experienced players?

LeBron answered those questions with a resounding "no" when he made his professional debut against the Sacramento Kings on October 29, 2003. In the first nine minutes of the game, he scored ten points, stole the ball, and assisted teammate Carlos Boozer on a slam dunk!

Moments after that assist, he raced the length of the court and threw down a dunk of his own, a monstrous right-handed tomahawk that would be featured over and over on the highlight reels. In all, James scored 25 points, ripped down 6 rebounds, dished 9 assists, and nabbed 4 steals. Those stats were the highest any prep-to-pro player had ever made in his first game. Not even Michael Jordan scored that many points in his debut.

As the season progressed, James continued to deliver outstanding performances, often earning double digits in more than one stat column. Despite this, the Cavs failed to win many games. On James's nineteenth birthday, December 30, they posted their twenty-second loss of the season.

If LeBron was frustrated, he did his best not to show it. Instead, he stepped up his game even more, hoping to pull his team out of the cellar.

Stepping up his game is exactly what he did the night of March 27, 2004. The Cavs were hosting the New Jersey Nets. Both teams had lost four of their last five games, but overall the Nets had the better record, with 42 wins and 30 losses to the Cavs' 32 wins and 42 losses.

LeBron entered the game determined that Cleveland would add another mark in its win column. While his shooting hand was cold early on — he took only four shots and made just one — he had three assists that put six points on Cleveland's side of the board. But by the end of the first quarter, New Jersey had racked up more points on their side, leading 28–24.

Then the second period began, and suddenly James found the hoop. He scored nine points, including a three-pointer, in just over two minutes! Unfortunately, he couldn't keep up the pace. Nor could his teammates. By halftime, the Nets had a ten-point lead. Another loss for the Cavs loomed on the horizon.

Or did it?

When the game resumed, LeBron went on a tear, scoring 11 points and passing for 4 assists. At the five-minute mark, he showed just how fired up he was by stealing the ball, dribbling madly to the other end, and slamming in a huge dunk. His play inspired his teammates to put the pedal to the metal. By the end of the third quarter, the Cavs had tightened the gap from 10 points to 3.

Unfortunately for Cleveland fans, the Nets once again took a commanding lead at the start of the last quarter. Their 3-point lead jumped to 5, to 7, and then to 11 with less than eight minutes left to go.

Once again, the Cavaliers looked poised for a loss.

Then something happened. In the middle of the fourth quarter, Cleveland began to score. In fact, they outscored the Nets 10–3 to tie it all up, 96–96, with less than four minutes remaining! The tying shot had come on a pass from LeBron. One free throw later, the Cavs had a single-point lead over the Nets.

Two minutes remained in the game. With the win suddenly in his sights, LeBron exploded, going on a scoring rampage. Boom! He drained a jump shot from nineteen feet out. Two points. Then he hit two free throws to bring his quarter total to four. Then, amazingly, in the last forty seconds he drove to the hoop three times for three more buckets — six, eight, *ten*! The last of these, a two-handed slam made with just two seconds on the clock, sealed the game for the Cavs, 107–104.

Those 10 points brought his game total to a career high of 41, making him the youngest rookie in NBA history to score 40 or more points in a single game. He also had a career high 13 assists, plus 6 rebounds and 3 steals, proving once more that for LeBron James, it was team first, self second.

"I hate losing," LeBron reminded the press after the game. Then he broke out into his mile-wide smile and added, "Oh, man, you know it was exciting!"

LeBron James was named Rookie of the Year following his stellar first season with the Cleveland Cavaliers. Since then, he has continued to achieve great success, almost single-handedly raising the team from cellar dwellers to the top of the ranks. In his rookie season, their record improved from 17–65 to 35–47. Two years later, they reached the playoffs, and in 2007 they made it all the way to the Finals for the first time in the team's history. That appearance ended in a loss to the Spurs, and the next year saw them bowing out in the semifinals. But with LeBron James in the lineup, the Cavs seem likely to show up in the postseason for many years to come.

★ JANUARY 22, 2006 ★

KOBE BRYANT

Chasing Wilt

When Wilt Chamberlain scored one hundred points in a single regulation game in 1962, no one thought any other player would ever break his record. And so far, nobody has. But in early 2006, someone came very, very close.

Kobe Bryant had been a member of the Los Angeles Lakers since 1996. In his rookie season, he was groomed to be the team's sixth man, their strong player off the bench. But he didn't stay on the bench for long.

While the young guard started just six games in the 1996–97 season and only a single match the following year, Kobe nearly doubled his minutes played in 1997–98, racking up incredible statistics during that time: 242 rebounds; 199 assists; 74 steals; 40 blocks; and an impressive 1,220 points, with an average of more than 15 per game!

Stats like that could not be ignored. When the

first match of the 1998–99 season was played in early February (the schedule was shortened due to disputes between the players and the league), Kobe was in the starting lineup. He drained 25 points that night, including 2 out of 3 three-pointers and 7 out of 9 free throws. In addition, he had 10 rebounds to give him his first double-double of the year. By season's end, he had increased his percentages in nearly all the stat columns.

It was the same in the years that followed. As Bryant grew more experienced, he became an increasingly important member of the Lakers' team. Together with big man Shaquille O'Neal and his other teammates, Kobe helped Los Angeles win the 2000 NBA Finals — and win again in 2001 and 2002. That "three-peat" cemented the Lakers as one of the all-time great basketball dynasties, alongside the Boston Celtics and the Chicago Bulls.

But as the saying goes, all good things must come to an end. Even before their third Finals victory, there had been rumors of strife between Kobe and Shaq. To the outside world, it appeared to be a case of "this town ain't big enough for the two of us." While both players publicly denied the rumors and offered words of support to each other, it was clear that any on-court chemistry they once had was gone. One of the star players would have to go. So, in the 2004 off-season, the Lakers made a difficult decision: they traded Shaq to the Miami Heat and kept Bryant.

It was a decision many soon questioned. Without Shaq in the lineup, the Lakers' record dropped from 56–36 in 2003–04 to 34–48 in 2004–05, their worst showing in years.

Yet the finger of blame could not be pointed at Kobe. Despite sitting out a month with a severe sprained ankle, he posted numbers equal to or better than those of the previous year. In fact, his average points per game jumped from 24 to 27.6. He had ten 40-plus-point games, and on April 20, 2005, he became the youngest player in the league to reach the 14,000-point milestone.

Still, Kobe realized that he needed to do even more. And he did — Kobe positively exploded offensively right from the beginning of the 2005–06 season. In each of his first four games, he scored 33 or more points! By the end of November, he had posted three 40-plus-point games. Then, on December 20 in a game against the Dallas Mavericks, he hit for an unbelievable 62 points — 22 free throws, 14 two-pointers, and 4 three-pointers — in just thirty-three minutes of play!

Few players have ever reached that number. Fewer still have topped it. Kobe is one of those people who have.

On January 22, 2006, the Lakers hosted the Toronto Raptors. The Raptors were trailing the Lakers in the standings, so many predicted a Los Angeles victory. But Toronto leaped out to an early lead and by the end of the first quarter was ahead, 36–29. Kobe had been responsible for 14 of the Lakers' points; he added 12 more in the second quarter. Yet nothing he did seemed to boost his team. At halftime, the Lakers trailed, 63–49.

According to Laker Lamar Odom, Bryant "was ticked off" by that 14-point deficit. "That's when it's bad," he added.

As in bad for the other team. When the Raptors and the Lakers met after the halftime break, Kobe Bryant had fire in his eyes and flames shooting from his fingertips. His accuracy went from good to absolutely phenomenal.

Two minutes into the third quarter, he made a layup. In the two minutes after that, he added 4 more points to the Lakers' side of the board. With

8:14 showing on the clock, he drained his second three-pointer of the night — and at 7:39 put in a third, and at 6:22 a fourth! In less than six minutes of play, Kobe had scored 15 points! His game total stood at 41, and there was still a quarter and a half left to go.

And yet, unbelievably, the Lakers were still behind, 75–65. So Kobe did the only thing he could do: he kept right on making baskets.

He hit an eighteen-foot jumper and was fouled. He made the free throw. Three points. Then he popped his fifth three-pointer through the hoop. Two more points followed, and then, with little more than a minute to go in the third quarter, he slammed down a dunk to give the Lakers their first lead of the game. Moments later, he thundered in a second dunk to end the quarter with an incredible 25 points!

And was he finished? He was not! Free throws, jump shots from inside and outside, and yet another set of back-to-back three-pointers — Kobe hit practically every shot he took! The fans were going insane, and the players, both Lakers and Raptors, were simply in awe.

"We were just watching him shoot," Chris Bosh of Toronto admitted.

"It's like a miracle unfolding in front of your eyes," Jerry Buss, owner of the Lakers, said of Kobe's spell-binding shooting.

When the final horn sounded and the dust settled, Kobe Bryant had racked up 81 points, the second-highest single-game total in the history of the league. The scoreboard said it all: Los Angeles 122, Toronto 104. Thanks to Kobe's smoking-hot hand, the Lakers had erased an 18-point deficit to *win* by 18 points!

"It's about the 'W,'" an exhausted but exuberant Kobe reminded the press after the game. "That's why I turned it on."

Had he ever imagined he would have a game like that? the media wanted to know.

"Not even in my dreams," he said. "To sit here and say I grasp what happened, that would be lying . . . and to put on a show like this for the fans here in L.A. is truly something special."

Kobe Bryant has continued to give Los Angeles fans "something special" since that night in 2006. While he hasn't bettered his 81-point game, he has had several 40-, 50-, and even a few 60-plus single-game totals. In 2008, he led his team back to the Finals, where he was targeted by the Boston Celtics and held for some of his lowest point totals of the season. But 2008 ended on a high note for him all the same: after several years of coming close, he finally received the league's coveted MVP award.

★ THE 2008 NBA FINALS ★

THE BOSTON CELTICS

On Top Again

The 2006–07 Boston Celtics were, in a word, embarrassing. The once-storied franchise, the team that had won more championships than any other, ended the regular season with just twenty-four wins. While it wasn't their worst record ever — ten years earlier they had won only fifteen — it was clear that if they were going to improve, changes needed to be made.

That's just what Danny Ainge, a former Celtics player and the current general manager, did. He already had one of the most consistent players in the league, the six-foot-five small forward Paul Pierce. A nine-year Celtics veteran, Pierce thrived on group effort. To bring out his best, therefore, Ainge would have to get players who were equally dedicated to teamwork. Those players, he believed, were Ray Allen and Kevin Garnett.

Guard Ray Allen had been in the NBA since 1996, playing first for the Milwaukee Bucks and then for the Seattle SuperSonics. He was an accurate three-point shooter and a top-notch playmaker. In his eleven-year career, he had been to the playoffs three times as a Buck and once with Seattle, but each time he had left ringless.

Thirty-year-old Kevin Garnett had played forward for the Minnesota Timberwolves since 1995. He had helped them reach the postseason eight consecutive times, from 1997–2004. The Timberwolves had failed to reach the Finals, however, and after their 2004 run, they had fallen behind in the standings. Their 2006–07 record was their worst in years.

Tired of supporting close-but-not-quite teams, Garnett and Allen were ready to make changes. After some negotiations, both agreed to leave the Western Division to come east and play for the Boston Celtics.

Almost from the beginning, Pierce, Allen, and Garnett — the "Big Three," as they were often called in memory of other famous Celtic trios — meshed like a finely tuned machine. Together with center Kendrick Perkins, point guard Rajon Rondo, and a strong supporting bench, they did what few people at the end of the last season thought possible for the Celtics. They won games — eight in a row, as a matter of fact, before dropping their first in mid-November!

That streak made basketball fans everywhere sit up and take notice. Were the Boston Celtics truly back, or were those wins just a fluke?

It was no fluke. In fact, according to some Celtics fans, it was a miracle. By the end of December, Boston had won 26 games and lost just 3. A month later, their record stood at 36–8. When the regular-season schedule concluded in April, the Celtics had won an unbelievable 66 games, while dropping only 12!

How much had Allen, Garnett, and Pierce con-tributed to those wins? A lot, as a glance at the game logs showed. Their names popped up over and over in the point-, assist-, and rebound-leader columns. Yet unlike so many star players, these three refused to put personal achievements ahead of their team. They even had a special word to describe their ded-ication to teamwork: *ubuntu*. Loosely translated from its Bantu origins, *ubuntu* means "I am, be-cause we are." In the context of sports, it means that a player is nothing without his team.

With *ubuntu* as their rallying cry, the Celtics made one of the greatest single-season turnarounds in NBA history. But now everyone wanted to know just one thing: would the team be able to sustain their momentum through the postseason, or would they collapse after having played so hard for so long?

First up in the playoffs was Altanta. It took the Celtics all seven games, but they finally clipped the Hawks' wings to advance to the second round. There they faced the powerful Cleveland Cavaliers and their superstar player, LeBron James. Once again, it took seven games, but Boston sent the Cavs riding home to watch the rest of the season from the sidelines. The Celtics caught a one-game break in their next series against the Detroit Pistons, winning that round in just six games.

Now, at long last, they were back in the NBA Finals and on the verge of reclaiming the title last won by the Celtics in 1986. All that stood in their way was their archrivals — the Los Angeles Lakers.

Behind the firepower of Kobe Bryant, the Lakers had posted a regular-season record of 57 wins and 25 losses. They had swept the Denver Nuggets in the first round of the playoffs, beaten the Utah Jazz 4–2, and beaten the San Antonio Spurs 4–1.

In all, the Lakers had played fifteen games in the postseason. The Celtics, on the other hand, had played twenty. Many wondered how they would hold up against the more rested Lakers.

They held up just fine, it turned out. The two teams were neck and neck throughout the first match, trading the lead back and forth. Then, midway through the third quarter, Kobe Bryant hit a running jumper to give Los Angeles a four-point advantage.

Moments later, disaster struck for the Celtics. Kendrick Perkins collided with Paul Pierce. Pierce hit the ground hard and clutched his right knee in agony. Play stopped while his teammates helped him off the floor. He disappeared into the locker room, leaving fans and teammates to face the grim possibility that he might not return.

The game resumed. Boston had managed to take a one-point lead when, suddenly, Pierce reemerged. His knee was taped, and he had a slight limp — but otherwise, he seemed fine!

A roar went up throughout the arena. No doubt plenty of fans were thinking of another game when an injured star returned and inspired his teammates to play their hearts out. That player was Willis Reed, and while Pierce later said he would never compare himself to Reed, he nevertheless inspired his team, just as Reed had nearly forty years earlier. When the final horn sounded, the Celtics had the win, 98–88.

They won game two as well, although they very nearly blew it. Going into the last quarter, Boston had a seemingly insurmountable 24-point lead. But all at once, the Lakers, led by a determined Kobe Bryant, went on a scoring rampage. They chalked up 31 points to the Celtics' 9!

With just twenty-two seconds left in the game, the score stood at 104–102. Then Paul Pierce drained two foul shots to make it 106–102. And when substitute forward James Posey hit two more, the Celtics had their second victory.

"We're happy because we won," Pierce told reporters after the game, "but we definitely learned a lesson."

The Celtics weren't happy after the following game, however — an 87–81 loss before crazed Los Angeles fans that saw Kobe Bryant hitting for 36 points.

Game four was nearly a duplicate of game two, only this time the Lakers were the ones who saw their huge 24-point advantage melt away before the

Celtics' heat. But where Boston had managed to hold on to their scant lead to win game two, Los Angeles had their lead overtaken in game four. End score: Boston 97, L.A. 91.

Boston needed just one more victory to win the championship. "Yeah," Kevin Garnett replied when asked if he thought the title was close, "I can taste it."

But the taste in the Celtics' mouth turned bitter in game five. Once more, the Lakers surged into the lead, going up by 19 points at one time. Boston battled hard to recover, but this time Los Angeles stood firm and won 103–98.

The series returned to Boston for game six. The stands in the TD Banknorth Garden were packed. Among the spectators were former Celtics greats John Havlicek, Bob Cousy, and Bill Russell. In the rafters above their heads fluttered the banners they had helped win so many years ago. There were sixteen in all, and if the Celtics — already the winningest team in NBA history — could win this night, they would add one more.

But a win was far from certain. The score seesawed throughout the first sixteen minutes of the game. Then, four minutes into the second quarter,

Los Angeles turned cold. They didn't make a single shot for more than two minutes. Boston, on the other hand, drained eleven to go up 43–29.

Los Angeles woke up after that, but their efforts were too little and, in the end, too late. Boston broke their lead wide open, from 11 to 17 to 21 to 30 to 36 until finally, with just half a minute left to go in the game, they were ahead by *39 points*!

The chant had long since begun: "Seven-TEEN! Seven-TEEN!" cried the fans as they stomped their feet in rhythm. Their cheers nearly drowned out the horn when the game clock ticked to zero. Final score: Boston 131, L.A. 92.

Paul Pierce, Ray Allen, Kevin Garnett, and the rest of the Celtics roared with glee. Garnett embraced his hero Bill Russell, saying, "I hope we made you proud."

Russell, whose first Finals win had come decades earlier, just smiled and replied, "You sure did."

Garnett had just one more thing to say before he hurried into the locker room. But he didn't just say it, he yelled it: *"That's that!"*

On October 28, 2008, the Boston Celtics played their 2008–09 season opener. Before the game, they raised their championship banner into the rafters. Paul Pierce wept openly, his pride at having achieved the ultimate basketball goal shining through his tears. "As a kid, I always dreamed of moments like this," Pierce told the crowd. "I've had a dream come true to add another banner to the rafters."

★ EPILOGUE ★

The Dream Team

Close your eyes and imagine a basketball team made up of the twelve best players of an era. Picture Magic Johnson sharing laughs with longtime rival and friend Larry Bird, and Scottie Pippen trading passes with John Stockton. Add "Sir" Charles Barkley, Karl "the Mailman" Malone, David "the Admiral" Robinson, and Clyde "the Glide" Drexler into the mix. Top it off with Patrick Ewing, Chris Mullin, and straight from Duke University, future NBA star Christian Laettner.

Oh, and Michael Jordan, of course.

A dream? No — the Dream Team.

In 1992, these twelve players were given a unique opportunity to represent the United States at the Summer Olympics in Barcelona, Spain. Unique, because it was the first time professional players were allowed to participate in the traditionally amateur games. A rule change in 1989 had opened the door for the sport's superstars to form a team. Those superstars jumped at the opportunity to play together and to introduce their style of basketball to the world.

How did the world's *other* basketball teams feel about facing the most dominant squad on Earth?

By all accounts, they were giddy with anticipation at just being on the same court with players they had never dreamed of meeting. They grabbed photos of themselves taken alongside Michael and the rest, sometimes off the court and sometimes, humorously, in the middle of a game! Sure, they all knew that they would likely be beaten by the United States, but these other teams didn't care.

"For us, the silver is the gold," quipped one coach.

There have been other Dream Teams since 1992, and each one has boasted the sport's top players. Shaquille O'Neal, Grant Hill, Hakeem Olajuwon, LeBron James, Allen Iverson, and many more have ably represented the United States in the last two decades. But interestingly, every Olympic year finds the United States facing stiffer competition.

Are other nations choosing better players? Possibly — but perhaps the answer lies in the fact that those nations glimpsed just how magical the sport could be when they saw the original Dream Team play. And, inspired, they worked to bring their own basketball programs in line with the best.

If so, then the sports world is a luckier place. Basketball is a game of graceful athleticism that is thrilling to experience and exciting to watch. That's something the original players back in 1891 realized, and every person to dribble, pass, and shoot a ball since has known.

In fact, when a basketball falls into the hands of a truly gifted player, it's enough to make one believe that humans were meant to fly after all.

Matt Christopher®

Sports Bio Bookshelf

Muhammad Ali	Randy Johnson
Lance Armstrong	Michael Jordan
Kobe Bryant	Peyton and Eli Manning
Jennifer Capriati	Yao Ming
Dale Earnhardt Sr.	Shaquille O'Neal
Jeff Gordon	Albert Pujols
Ken Griffey Jr.	Jackie Robinson
Mia Hamm	Alex Rodriguez
Tony Hawk	Babe Ruth
Ichiro	Curt Schilling
LeBron James	Sammy Sosa
Derek Jeter	Tiger Woods

THE #1 SPORTS SERIES FOR KIDS ®

Read them all!

*Previously published as Crackerjack Halfback

All available in paperback from Little, Brown and Company
**Previously published as Pressure Play
***Previously published as Baseball Pals